About the Author

Liz Syred was born in Scotland and spent much of her teenage years and adulthood in England with her family until relocating to Inverness in 2004 with her husband and young son.

Most of her career was spent in the Civil Service in London. On moving to the Highlands, she worked in the voluntary sector and for five years worked for Connecting Carers, the Carer Centre for Highland.

Popping In

Liz Syred

Popping In

Olympia Publishers
London

www.olympiapublishers.com
OLYMPIA PAPERBACK EDITION

A CIP catalogue record for this title is
available from the British Library.

ISBN: 978-1-78830-599-0

This is a work of creative nonfiction. The events are portrayed to the
best of the author's memory. While all the stories in this book are
true, some names and identifying details have been changed to
protect the privacy of the people involved.

First Published in 2020

Olympia Publishers
Tallis House
2 Tallis Street
London
EC4Y 0AB

Printed in Great Britain

Dedication

I dedicate this book to everyone who find themselves devoting their lives to support their loved ones, and as a result, many of whom have not been able to follow their own personal dreams and ambitions. In particular thank you to all the carers I met while working at Connecting Carers, who shared their lives with me and especially the carers at the Inverness Drop-In who suggested the idea of this book and who encouraged me to write it.

To my husband, Richard, and son, Dominic, for believing in me, encouraging me in everything I do and for patiently listening to me talk about the stories and plan for *Popping In*.

Acknowledgements

Thank you to everyone who has supported me in this venture. In particular, Karen Anderson, who did an amazing job proofreading as well as share stories that she, as a carer, was happy for me to include.

To Sandra Bain and Debbie Thompson who spent hours going through the script and encouraging me.

To Roisin Connelly, Manager of the Highland Carer Centre – Connecting Carers for all her support and encouragement to get the story published and for giving her time to sit and read the script even though she had so much going on in her own life at the time.

And finally, last but not least, my husband, Richard for just being him, for loving, encouraging and believing in me as well as all the hours he spent reading and checking my grammar in real 'teacher style' — red pen in hand.

Chapter 1

"You! I need a drink. Where's my drink?" a voice called out.

Rachel stood looking at herself in the bathroom mirror. *When did you move from being 'Rachel darling', to simply 'You'?* she asked herself as she gazed into the empty brown eyes facing her.

Is this a crazy dream? Is my past catching up with me or, is it true that it happens to one in three people these days? Rachel mused cynically as she brushed her teeth.

The muttering and banging continued and she knew she could no longer hide away. She glanced at the lilac leather make-up bag sitting on the side where it had lain for days. She walked past it. *What's the point? He doesn't even notice whether I'm wearing make-up nowadays. No matter how much you paint it on girl it won't cover up the pain and loneliness that's sucking life out of you.* She drew herself back from her thoughts.

"I'm coming dear," Rachel called, desperately trying to be bright and cheerful but all the while hearing the tense pitch in her voice as she walked towards the kitchen where John, her husband, was standing.

"Hey. You! Where's my breakfast? I'm thirsty, and I need a cup of tea," he barked as he lifted and dropped the kettle then the cereal bowl onto the kitchen surface. He shuffled about opening and closing drawers and banging doors. "Where is it? Where is it? What have you done with my money?" he yelled out, as he frantically rummaged around, getting louder and more aggressive with each thump.

Rachel smiled and interrupted calmly, "It's OK John, your money is safe. It's in the bank. Remember? We talked about this yesterday and I showed you the bank statement and everything."

She walked closer to him and gently took his hand in hers. "Come on John, come and sit down and I'll get that tea and breakfast for you. There's not enough room in here for both of us and you know I make a better cup of tea than you," she said jesting.

He stopped and looked round at her. For a brief moment, she was convinced she'd seen a glimmer of recognition flicker in his eyes. Hope rose in her heart, but as quickly as it came, it was dashed. The scowl she had come to recognise was back and he just glared at her.

"Who are you? What are you doing here? Don't think you can come in here and take the place of my Rachel. I won't have it. Do you hear?" By this time, he had picked up the bread knife that had been left on the side.

Rachel noticed the knife immediately and began to panic. She thought she had put that away last night but realised she must have forgotten. She had to get John settled into his chair and give him his medication or things could all too easily escalate out of control.

"No, John. I'm not here to take Rachel's place, I'm just here to help." She remembered the doctor saying not to argue with him about who she was. "Come and sit down and let's have a cup of tea. You said you were thirsty." She edged toward him, a fake smile forming on her face and her bottom lip beginning to quiver. Tears pricked her eyes as she watched intently what he was doing with the knife. *Damn. Why had she left it out in the first place?*

He looked round and gazed directly into her face, his vivid blue eyes softening and becoming bright. "Oh hello. Did you say a cup of tea? Wonderful. Thank you." With that he dropped the knife on the counter and walked past her into the lounge, taking his place in his lazy-boy chair opposite the TV. Totally unconcerned he picked up the remote and started flicking through the TV channels.

Rachel felt her body go limp as the tension seeped away slowly. She switched on the kettle and started to make his porridge. Yes, there was a routine that had to be followed. He always had porridge, followed by toast, marmalade and tea, as he had done for the past twenty years.

Having enjoyed his breakfast and taken his medication without any difficulty, John, now settled, dozed off to sleep.

Mmm, that's one good thing; he seems to trust me with his medication, Rachel thought as she gently covered John with his tartan plaid to keep him warm and snug. As she tucked in the blanket, she tenderly stroked his cheek. *He had once been such a clever man, full of life and fun and so caring. Why does it have to be like this? I always thought dementia happened to people who weren't clever, who ate unhealthy diets and didn't use their brain. Not to someone with John's talents.* Tears welled up and flowed down her cheeks. Tears were never far away these days. Not only did the sadness of the current situation overwhelm her from time to time, but it always came with a deep, sickening pain in the pit of her stomach, taking her back to what seemed like light years ago, to a time in her life from which she thought she had permanently escaped.

No. I'm not going there, I won't give in to that, I can't. I must be strong. I must be here for John like he was for me at a time I most needed him. Standing up, she fumbled in her sleeve for her hanky, and drying her tears she picked up the remote, switched the TV off, and gathered up the dishes, wandering back into the kitchen.

I have to keep myself busy or I'll go crazy, she thought to herself and purposefully pulled down a recipe book to make a cake for John.

***

Louise Sinclair had been busy weaving in and out of shops, offices and anywhere she could find to stick up a poster about the Pop-In for carers. She had been working with the charity, LifeLine, for eight months, and was enthusiastic and determined to help every carer she could find. The Pop-In was the favourite part of her job and she wanted to see the coffee shop full of carers.

The Pop-In had been meeting every Tuesday for the past two years. On average, ten to fifteen people attended each week but Louise knew without a doubt so many more people could be helped by it. The group was such a disparate mix of people. When she reflected upon the stories she had listened to over the past few months it was amazing how resilient they all were.

As she emerged from the library, she smiled recalling the faces of those who had confided in her about their situations. She was intrigued how they had found a way to accept their lot and not become bitter. How could they laugh and support one another, and not resent people around them? As a result of all this Louise was resolute. She was going to do her best to be available for them, supporting them any way she could. And with that she strode off back to the car.

Louise had an appointment with a carer and she must not be late. This gentleman had contacted the charity a while ago asking for help. He was bewildered and desperately lonely. He had been widowed and was now the carer for his adult son. The lad had significant learning difficulties and had not coped with the death of his mum.

Louise trundled along in her old banger. With her sat-nav directing her she was able to stop thinking about the route to her destination which gave her space to think about the background information she had been given about another carer. How sad is that situation. Is there anyone out there having an ordinary, non-dramatic life? Oops, missed the turning,

"Oi, sat-nav woman you are too slow. I've missed the turning now. Oh bother."

'Please turn around as soon as possible and take the next turning on the right.'

"Yeah, OK, I heard you," Louise mumbled and swept the car round in the middle of the road, switching sat-nav woman to mute. "I wonder how many other people shout at their sat-nav? I can't believe I'm the only one," she said aloud within the confines of her old red Micra — her pride and joy! She had decorated the bonnet and doors with bright yellow tulip stickers! There was no chance Louise (or anyone else for that matter) would miss this car.

Louise found Mr Walford's house and, gathering up her papers and leaflets etc., she walked along the drive and rang his doorbell.

***

Rachel had finished making the walnut and coffee cake for John and it was sitting on the work surface ready for him. She had made his bed and generally tidied up their little home. It was such a lovely place.

"Darling, you must come and see this beautiful little house I've found for us," she recalled John saying. The tenderness and excitement in his voice was still as clear today as it had been when John brought her to Inverness twenty years previously. And, as soon as she had walked into the house she had known she had come home. For the first time in her life she felt she belonged, was loved and she had a future.

As she made the single bed in what had once been their bedroom, the loneliness shrouded her once again. She recalled the nights they had lain together, entwined in each other's arms promising to be this close and loving when they grew old together. She winced as she walked into what had once been the spare room but was now her bedroom. Rachel sat on the edge of her bed. *I must find life beyond these four walls,* she thought to herself, something outside of just being John's carer. *Otherwise I'm going to go crazy. I have to accept John will never draw me close, hold me in his arms and kiss me with passion or desire again. Yet I'm his wife and I promised 'in sickness and in health.' It all seemed so trivial and irrelevant then.*

With an aching and heavy heart, she rose and went through to the lounge where John was stirring. "Fancy a cup of tea and a piece of coffee and walnut cake, dear? I've made it fresh for you."

With that John looked up, smiled and said, "That'd be lovely, perhaps then we could sit and watch a film together?"

"Oh yes, what a wonderful idea." Rachel turned and skipped through to the kitchen, made a pot of tea and cut the cake. With her heart feeling much lighter, she returned to the lounge with the tray, smiling and ready to sit with John. "Please, please God," she prayed, "please, please don't let anything spoil this. Just this afternoon. Give me this afternoon that's all I ask."

***

Louise was more determined than ever to seek out carers who were isolated and lonely. She remembered being told when she started this job that in the Highland area alone there was somewhere in the region of twenty-seven thousand unpaid carers, yet Lifeline only worked with about two thousand of those so far! She jumped in her car and checked her diary. *Oh good,* she thought, *no more appointments today. I know what I'm going to do, I'm going to get you sat-nav woman to choose the next five streets on my way home and I'll push flyers about the Pop-In through each door.* And with that she set off.

Blantyre Street. "Mmm this looks promising," and no sooner said Louise parked the car, pulled out the flyers and set off down the street. "This is going to be great. I can just see people picking up the flyer and resolving to come to the Pop-In. Well OK, some might and maybe others will contact us for help or perhaps tell us of folk they know who need help." Anyway, it was a good start and she wasn't going to be defeated. Raising her head, Louise strode up to the next door in the row of terraced houses. Back in the car she moved on to the second and third streets, well pleased with herself. As she glanced at the pile of flyers lying on the passenger seat, she realised she was running low and would therefore only have enough for one more street. As she parked, she noticed that each of the houses along the road were small cottage-style houses. "I wonder if these are for older folk or possibly sheltered accommodation? They could all be potential customers for the Pop-In." With that she scooped up the last of the flyers and shot up one side of the road and down the other with great gusto. Now she could go home content in the knowledge that she had had a profitable day.

***

Rachel was suddenly aware of music playing. On opening her eyes, she was in time to see the closing credits of the film. Oh my, I've been asleep through most of the film. Glancing round at John she found him staring at the screen with a serene smile on his face.

As she went to get out of her chair she realised she had been very relaxed and that her earlier prayer had been answered and nothing had spoiled it. "Well that was lovely, wasn't it, John? Fancy another cuppa?" She walked over to him and took his cup.

"Yes, You, I'll have another cup of tea. You said you were going to get it ages ago and you just went off and left me here waiting for you. Three buses have passed while I've been waiting for you. Now it's too late." With that he turned his face toward the wall.

Rachel silently walked out of the room into the kitchen and filled the kettle. She smiled to herself and muttered, "It was nice while it lasted. Perhaps tomorrow will be a good day."

At that she heard the letterbox click. She walked to the front door and found a flyer sticking through the slot. Pulling it out Rachel read: 'LifeLine — Are you an unpaid carer? Then this could be for you. Come and join us at 'Chinwags' in Chapel Gardens each Tuesday morning.' "I wonder what that's all about? A Pop In? I wonder if it's something I could go along to? Maybe this could help me. Oh, I don't know. I probably wouldn't fit in. I haven't been anywhere socially on my own for such a long time now, I don't think I'd know what to say or do." She crumpled up the flyer and went to throw it in the box for recycling, but at that the kettle clicked and she turned to fill the teapot and unconsciously dropped the flyer on the top of the fridge and carried on with making the tea.

"You! Where are you? I need you to get me the remote. Where's my tea? Oi, You, what do you think you are doing?"

Rachel picked up the tray and traipsed back into the lounge. "That's it," Rachel said aloud. "Thanks, John, I think you've just made up my mind. I'll seriously think about this Pop-In." Smiling she walked over to John.

Chapter 2

Hot and flustered Louise charged along, down the lane and into Chapel Gardens towards Chinwags Café. "Oh, I'll bet I'm late again. I really need to leave earlier so as to miss the school buses. I can't believe they have to go that slow," she muttered to herself. "What a relief the lights aren't on yet and the doors still locked." With that she dropped onto an outside bench and gave out a massive sigh, her breath floating away as if she had puffed a cigarette. "Oh good, it gives me time to check my phone to see if anyone's left a message to say they aren't going to make it to the Pop-In today."

Every Tuesday Louise turned up at the café ready to host the Pop-In for carers. This was their group, and time for them to come along for a couple of hours to 'chill out', chat, laugh and have a coffee. This provided them a little respite away from their caring role, allowing them to put their concerns and worries aside for a brief while.

The sun was shining in the clear blue sky. A few fluffy clouds went meandering by. One could have been mistaken for thinking it was going to be a warm, sunny day if it hadn't been for the definite autumn 'nip' in the air. At last the large wooden door creaked open and it was Margaret, clutching a rather garish noticeboard signposting passers-by to 'Chinwags Community Café', a very welcoming sight.

Louise jumped up dropping her phone in her handbag whilst simultaneously grabbing hold of the hessian shopping bag sitting on the bench.

"Hi Margaret. Am I glad to see you?" Louise said, greeting her with a warm smile. "It's a lovely day, but a bit chilly for sitting around too long."

"Aye, it is too. I have to say though I do love this time of year; all the colours in the leaves, the low mist resting on the mountains and the clean, crisp fresh air. Oh, dearie me, I sound like an advert! But autumn is my favourite time of year. I got married forty years ago next week, and I'm still alive and able to tell the tale," she laughed.

"I can't believe it. Where does time go?" Margaret held the door open for Louise to walk inside ahead of her.

"I still feel like a young woman starting out, content and happily married. Not sure Iain would say he was happy, but am quite sure he is content. Content enough for me to be running around after him that's for sure;" Margaret chuckled.

"Forty years! That's a lifetime," Louise responded. "It must be really nice being with someone that long, I just can't imagine it myself."

"Oh, you will lass, when the time is right. One day some handsome prince will walk into your life, sweep you off your feet and you'll just know he is 'the one.'" Margaret laughed, and walking toward the kitchen she called over her shoulder, "but do you want to know the secret to making it last? Hard work, determination and compromise!"

Having lived all her life in Inverness, Louise had watched her tight-knit community grow from a bustling town into a thriving city. It had been a place where everybody knew everyone; extended families stayed close supporting each other. Neighbours had grown up and shared lives together. Yet, as the town had expanded and 'newcomers' had moved in, the very fabric of the community was changing. And for many folk, it was not necessarily for the better.

Many, especially young people, went away to university and college and never came back, seeking their fortunes and careers further afield. From Louise's point of view the 'Gateway to the Highlands' had opened up lots of opportunities and prosperity in the region. However, she was particularly aware that with expansion came change, bringing new challenges. Loneliness was one such challenge.

Louise loved this building, often imagining the people who had lived and worked here. It was very old. A plaque hung over the front door: "General Wolfe, Victor of Quebec attended The Boys Grammar School here."

Every time Louise walked through the door she heard her Grannie's voice in her head, "Your great, great, great Grannie was one of the few girls to attend the first female school in this very building."

Today Louise smiled and muttered under her breath "Mmm, wonder if my great, great, great Grannie flirted with General Wolfe. Now that is a thought!" And it was one that made her smile!

However, this lovely old building had recently been renovated. Margaret had created a beautifully cosy environment that offered support and friendship to the growing number of people who were lonely and in need of a helping hand. Indeed, Chinwags had exceeded its ambition, with people from all walks of life across Highland drawn to the restored building. The Pop-In was only a small part of what was on offer there, but its role was highly significant to those who attended each week.

Louise called out, "Margaret the place looks lovely today. You've done an amazing job with the tables. I love the brightly coloured tablecloths. You're amazing! I sometimes wish I was like you; able to make even the simplest things look special." Everywhere there were small traces of Margaret's creative talent and love for her customers. Simple touches became works of art in her hands.

Margaret was such good fun. She had a larger-than-life jolly personality. Her face was always glowing, which wasn't just from cooking her speciality scones or the glow of the open fire, but largely due to her generally happy and warm disposition that simply emanated a love for people. She, and her dedicated team of staff, made everyone feel welcome. They lavished tea, coffee and delicious home baking on all who walked in. Staff would seek out anyone on their own chatting to them, endeavouring to ensure no-one who entered left the cafe feeling lonely, unwanted or under-valued.

When Louise first took over hosting the group, she had been concerned that the get-together would be a 'moaning meeting' where discussion would be all about how bad things were and about the perceived inefficiency of social services staff. But, in fact, the opposite had been true. Yes, there were of course times of sadness when one person would arrive upset. However, they would talk, and sometimes shout about it, but everyone would listen, offer support, someone would share a joke or a funny story and the mood would revert back to general banter.

The open fire in the large stone hearth facing the door was starting to heat up providing a warm welcome from the cold day outside. Throughout the autumn and winter months a roaring fire could always be seen heating the hearth. On either side on the fireplace piles of chopped wood were stacked suggesting to all who entered that the fire would never fade.

Having made her way to the long table in the middle of the room, Louise slid off her coat and threw it over the back of her chair, just as the door opened and in walked Mollie.

"Morning," Mollie called out.

She dropped her bags, "Just popping to the loo. I need a mirror to sort my hair. It's a right mess and I can't take my hat off until I fix it. I can't let anyone see me like this. I'll be back in a mo."

Mollie trotted off through the pine door, hairbrush in hand. Louise smiled. She was very fond of Mollie, who'd been very kind when she had taken on responsibility of the Pop-In.

Mollie emerged from the toilet, silvery grey hair now suitably in place and took her seat opposite Louise. They looked round in time to see Annabel walk through the door.

"I cannae believe it. Whit am I supposed to dae? It disnae matter whit I do or whit I tell them, naebody believes me. If they're no on at me aboot one thing or another, and I jist didnae understand whit they're on aboot," Annabel said as she walked towards Louise and Mollie, clearly in a great deal of pain.

"So what's happened now?" asked Louise. She had tried to persuade the single mum to 'take a back seat' and not respond to every demand her family put on her.

"You just won't believe it. I'm so angry, upset and tired. I jist don't hae the energy to keep fightin' for whit Josie needs. I ken she's an adult and jist finished Uni, but I dinae seem to be able to get Social Services to understand she still needs support to handle things."

"Have you spoken with Advocacy to see if they can help? I know in the past my husband and I found them very helpful and it gave us confidence to state our case," Mollie suggested gently.

"Aye, I've called and left a message asking someone to call me, but to be honest Josie knows what she needs and has telt them whit she wants. Och I get so frustrated when I feel no-one's listening. It's as though they've already decided whit Josie does and doesnae need. And one thing they think she doesnae need is an interfering mither! But it's no that. I've worked so hard at no being over protective, or pushy, especially when she went away to Uni. Josie's achieved so much which has really boosted her confidence. She's so much potential, but she still needs some support. I jist want the best for her so she doesn't lose what she's achieved. Surely that is no different to any other mither!"

Margaret arrived at the end of the table.

"Hello ladies. Do you want to order your drinks now or wait till the others arrive?" The three looked at each other and hesitated. Louise piped up, "Oh, I think we'll wait a few minutes just to see if the others arrive, if that's OK?"

"Yes, fine," replied Margaret, and wandered off back into the kitchen.

"I've had a terrible week." Annabel announced. "Louise, can you hae a look at this. It's a letter I've received from the JobCentre. I canna understand whit they're saying. Surely, they ken there's no way I can work. My doctor's already telt them. Are they goin' to stop my benefits? I cannae manage as it is." Annabel's voice became faster and more agitated.

"Let me have a look at the letter," Louise replied calmly. "I'm sure everything will be fine."

"Maybe we should have our coffee now." She turned and called out to Margaret.

On reading the letter Louise established that Annabel had been invited to an interview to discuss whether she was able to return to work. The new Work Programme with its changes to the benefit system was being piloted in Inverness and it was definitely impacting on lives of folk in the Highlands.

Over the next ten minutes the door continued to open and shut while others in the group arrived, including Jackie who burst in laughing and chatting to those who walked in with her.

Margaret returned to the table and started taking orders.

"Your usual, Annabel, — tea, toast and marmalade? Yes?" Margaret reeled off.

"Aye that wid be lovely, thank you Margaret" replied Annabel.

Margaret moved onto Mollie, "And I assume you want black coffee and a Tunnock's tea cake, Mollie?"

"Yes, right again, Margaret. Thanks. It would throw you if I changed my mind one of these days and had a hot chocolate and some carrot cake, wouldn't it?"

"Oh, talking of carrot cake," piped up Louise, "that'll do me nicely. Thanks. With a nice cuppa."

Because of Margaret's amazing memory everyone got what they wanted and the chat moved on both effortlessly and seamlessly.

Jackie placed her order and then announced, "Oh, I have something to read that will gi' you all a laugh," and with that she buried her head in her handbag while everyone started to drink their tea or coffee waiting in expectation for her to continue.

"Here it is. I cut it out of my magazine at the weekend and it made me laugh. Let's put the seniors in the jail," she began, "and the criminals in nursing homes. That way the seniors would have access to showers, hobbies and walks. They'd receive unlimited free prescriptions and receive money instead of paying out!..."

Everyone laughed and that started a conversation as to whether prisoners should have rights!

"I think it would be really funny seeing all the old folk wearing prison uniform. What do you think, Mollie? You wouldn't have to worry about your hair then, would you?" Francesca shouted out laughing heartily.

"Oh, I don't know about that," Mollie replied. "I'd probably worry about it more because of the constant video monitoring and guards checking on me every twenty minutes. I'd be brushing it all the time and probably end up with no hair."

Everyone chuckled and the conversation continued.

Annabel stood up and putting on her coat, announced

"Louise I've got tae go now. I need tae go to the Citizen's Advice Bureau wi' my letter and see if I can get them to sort things for me. I just cannae dae it on my own."

"OK Annabel, you do that. Just remember, take your time and listen to what they say. You might find it helpful if you were to write things down. What do you think?" asked Louise.

"Aye, I'll try and I'll gie yi a call later to let yi know how I got on, eh!" Annabel responded.

"That's fine with me". Louise smiled. "Take care." With that Annabel made her way out the door.

Louise turned and said, "Mollie, how do you cope with your son? Do you have to deal with some of the issues Annabel faces?"

Mollie smiled, "I can't believe I've been a carer for over forty years. Where has that time gone? It doesn't seem possible. Nobody tells you when you set sail into the sunset with your Merchant Navy officer exploring so many different places around the world, that all too soon you might become an unpaid carer for the rest of your life.

"One memory that stands out, was when my husband arranged for me and our two boys to join him on the ship. We left here to make our way on the train. Two small boys and loads of luggage. We were OK this end but when we got to Edinburgh and had to change trains it was a nightmare. I remember it was rush hour and the station was really busy. Standing on the platform, I pondered how I was going to get the luggage and the boys on board and find our seats. The swarm of commuters just kept barging past. Fortunately, three young students came along and asked if they could help and very kindly took the luggage on to the train whilst the boys and I found our seats. I've never forgotten that and have always had a soft spot for students ever since because they really seemed to care."

The morning passed quickly enough and soon it was coming up to 11:30am. People came and went. The door opened again and in walked Caroline. She wandered round saying 'hi' to everyone, and Margaret appeared with a steaming hot chocolate for her.

"Just what I need Margaret, thank you," Caroline declared.

She then sat down next to Mollie in what had been Annabel's seat. Looking rather distressed Caroline peeled off her coat. Mollie turned and enquired gently,

"Caroline what's happened?" At that, tears filled Caroline's eyes and she tried to sip the hot chocolate, hoping her tears would be dried away by the steam floating up into her face.

"Oh I don't know. It's just everything getting on top of me I guess. Alison wants to move again, and Angus is just as bad." Caroline said. "She doesn't want to live in that place anymore, but it will be the same again. That one will never be settled, that's for sure." Caroline uttered despondently.

Louise patted Caroline's shoulder. She understood. For Caroline, her children were her life. Not only was she their mum, she'd been, and still was her daughter's carer and she had never stopped blaming herself for passing on the genetic condition that both she and Alison lived with. Fortunately, Angus being male was lucky, he was immune. He was a lovely lad, very fond of his mum and sister and did what he could to help. In his own way, he always felt guilty that he had been fortunate not to suffer like his mum and his twin sister.

Throughout the morning, Louise moved around the group making sure she had spoken to everyone,

"Remember it's the book club next week, so bring back your books," she called out down the table.

Louise's mobile phone rang. She charged round the table and quickly grabbed it.

"Hi, Louise here," she said into the phone.

"Louise, just to let you know we have had a new enquiry from a carer called Rachel Norris. She got our contact details from a flyer pushed through the door and she's interested in attending the Pop-In next week."

"Oh wow, that's great. Worth all that traipsing around," Louise quickly jotted down the lady's contact details. "Thanks, that's so good. I'll give her a call and encourage her to come along."

It was time to wrap things up. The group started to disperse. The young mums wandered off together, chatting and laughing as they went. After saying goodbye to the last of the group, Louise scooped up her bags, thanked Margaret and the girls and set off back to the carpark.

Strolling back to the car, two hours after her arrival, Louise mused over the conversations of the morning; the concerns and questions folk had expressed. The number of problems and difficulties people faced on a daily basis was truly incredible and yet they dealt with them, supported each other and got on with life. She was so blessed and she wondered how she would cope with life if it had handed her any of the situations those in the group lived with day after day. She thought about Annabel and hoped her meeting with the CAB had been successful.

As she crossed the street towards the car park, Louise made a mental note to phone those who hadn't been there today to make sure they were OK. She missed them when they were absent.

"Oh, I'd better get a move on or I'll be rushing again and late for my next appointment and that won't do".

En-route, she decided to drop into the library and pick up the books for next week's book club, hoping that the choice for this coming month would be more interesting than the last month's offering had been!

Chapter 3

A week had passed since Rachel had picked up the flyer about the Chinwags Pop-In. In fact, every day since that afternoon, she had picked it up, looked at it and put it back on top of the fridge, each time muttering, "Just throw it out, Rachel, you know you're not going to go. Who's going to want to talk to you and what will you talk about anyway?"

Yet, something inside prevented her from actually throwing it in the re-cycle bin. Perhaps it was the deep desire that she would find friendship, someone to talk to or perhaps it was just pure desperation.

Rachel smiled to herself as she recalled the conversation at the end of last week with the young girl who had called from LifeLine. She had been so friendly and made her feel that she was genuinely cared for. The girl had seemed so excited that someone had read her leaflet.

She finished clearing up the dishes. John was washed, dressed and had had his breakfast and was now sitting in his chair with the TV Times balanced on his lap. *I'll give him his medication just before I leave,* Rachel thought to herself. *That way he'll be settled and I'll be back before he gets restless.*

It'll also provide me with a good excuse to leave early if I don't like the group or it becomes too overwhelming.

Picking up the wash bag, Rachel quickly put some make-up on and made herself presentable. With one last look in the mirror, she picked up her handbag and jacket and took them through to the hall leaving them by the front door. She didn't want to agitate John and she knew she had to play the goodbye very carefully, so she walked into the kitchen for the medication and wandered slowly through into the lounge.

"Darling, here are your tablets. Can you take them now for me please?"

She placed the pills in his hand as she spoke. Rachel held her breath waiting to see if he was going to start arguing with her, but he looked up at her, took them and dropped them straight in his mouth. Rachel quickly handed him a glass of water and in no time at all the deed was done.

"You, turn on the TV. I want to watch the news."

Rachel, eager to please, snatched up the remote and pressed the channel button for News 24. She smiled at him and placed the remote back on the side table next to him.

"Well, John, I'm just popping out for a short while. I won't be long, you just sit there and relax."

She covered his legs with the tartan blanket. John was already engrossed with the news and didn't even notice that she had gone. Picking up her jacket and bag she quietly stepped out into the fresh air.

Rachel found her way to the café and as she turned into the street she saw a notice advertising Chinwags — The Community Café. Her heart started thumping. She turned hot and cold but continued walking ever closer toward the garish sign, feeling as though she was being drawn by some supernatural presence.

Arriving at the large wooden door she took a deep breath and pushed it open and walked in. It was busy, very warm and exuded a friendly, happy atmosphere: bustling with lots of laughing and chatting. There, at a long table in the middle of the room, sat a group of people, various ages, male and female, all with a mug and cake in front of them. Rachel hesitated and suddenly panic rose within her. 'I can't do this I have to get out. This was such a mistake.'

But as she turned to go, she heard someone call out and appear at her side.

"Hello. Are you Rachel? Are you here for the Pop-In?

"Eh, yes," Rachel stammered.

"Oh, that's great. I'm Louise. I spoke with you on the phone the other day. I'm so glad you've made it. Here, come with me and I'll introduce you to the group. You'll have a great time. It's lovely to have you."

With that they walked over to the long table and Mollie moved along to the next chair so that Rachel could join the group and sit close to Louise.

She sat down smiling and nodding at each face in turn as Louise went around the table introducing everyone. Rachel knew she wouldn't remember all their names but was suddenly aware that for the first time in a long time she was beginning to relax. The warm cosy atmosphere surrounded her, and the friendly faces of everyone gathered there made her feel welcome. In an instant, she knew she was accepted. Margaret appeared by her side.

"What would you like to drink?"

"Oh, a cup of tea would be lovely, if that's OK?"

"Certainly, and can I interest you in one of our freshly baked scones, a slice of carrot cake or a tea cake?"

"Oh, a tea cake, please." With that Rachel started to rummage in her bag for her purse to pay for her tea and cake.

"Oh, Rachel, you don't have to worry about that, we pay for the refreshments. We want to spoil you a little, so just enjoy it."

Rachel dropped her purse back in her in bag and pushed it under the table in front of her.

"Louise, I have tae tell you what happened when I went tae see Citizens Advice Bureau and then the Jobcentre. I'm just so glad I went tae CAB first. They were so helpful. I wid never hae got anywhere wi the Jobcentre if it had nae been for the lad at CAB. The lassie at the Jobcentre said she does nae want to see me fir another three months. I dinae ken why they think I'll be able to work in three months when I hae this genetic disease and arthritis. The medical report says I'll never be fit fir work. I think the lassie must believe in miracles or something. Anyway, we'll just hae to wait and see."

"Don't worry, Annabel, it will all come right in the end. The fact that you have someone at CAB who is helpful and understanding is a big thing. They will guide you with how to manage the folk at the Jobcentre. Anyone in their right mind can see you are not ready for work so don't worry. After all, if you do return to work you are only going to make your condition worse and then where will you be?"

Louise went on, "And you need to look after yourself or who will be there for Josie?"

Louise worried about Annabel. She was such a gentle soul, caring and kind to everyone. The group was her rescue and escape route and she could always be relied upon to be there health permitting. In many ways, her daughter was very demanding and took advantage of her good nature but there was no point in trying to persuade her to step back because her daughter was all she had and she felt responsible - and needed - and that was paramount in her thinking.

"Oh, here, I've another funny story to tell you," Jackie jumped in. "I could nae believe it this morning. I was standing at the bus stop and a lady that I've become friends with because we are always standing waiting for a bus, came along. We were chatting when the bus drove up. The pair of us got on and said 'hello' to the other five or so folk on the bus. We sat down and off went the bus. Suddenly the bus driver piped up and asked if any of us knew the way to the Retail Park. Everyone looked at each other. 'Why are we going to the Retail Park? That's no' the bus route. Has the route changed?' I shouted out to the driver, and he said ,'yes, due to the fire on the main route buses are being diverted and I'm not sure where I'm going.'

"There was uproar. Everyone just fell about laughing believing the bus driver was having a joke with us. However, it soon became clear he wasn't. He really was lost. It all came tumbling out that he had only started in the job the week before and had been shown the regular route. However, this fire meant everything was diverted and no-one had shown him where to go and so he was totally confused. Can yae believe that? We all felt so sorry for him and so one of the passengers walked up to the driver's cabin and directed him through town. It was hilarious," said Jackie.

"Anyway, we got here and it was such a laugh. Mind you I'm not sure what happened when we all eventually got off the bus. There will probably be an article in The Courier about a bus driver last seen driving up the A9 towards John O'Groats."

Folk laughed and that started everyone sharing journeys on trains, buses and even planes. Rachel sat quietly watching and listening. Some of the stories made her smile and once or twice she caught herself actually giggling a bit. That had become so unusual it brought her up sharp. She hadn't entirely lost all her sense of humour she realised, it had simply become buried.

The topic of conversation shifted again, and as Rachel listened she realised she wasn't the only one with heartbreak and a stressful life. *These people are just like me. Mm, they seem to be coping better than me. That lady Jackie is funny, quite the life and soul of the group it would appear.*

Penny was sitting discreetly watching Rachel. Penny was curious as to whom Rachel cared for but didn't want to pry. She could tell Rachel was nervous but she seemed a really kind and pleasant person. Penny knew from her own experience that the Pop-In could be really valuable to so many people.

"Rachel, I'm really glad you came today. Do you live in town?" Penny asked.

"Er no, I'm not in town but not that far away, just up in Blantyre Street." Rachel smiled, averted her eyes in the hope Penny wouldn't ask any further questions."

But Penny understood how Rachel was feeling and knew how important it was that she got a chance to talk. Penny remembered if it hadn't been for Francesca talking to her the first day she had attended the Pop-In she would never have returned. Louise had been lovely but having someone who really understood how she felt had proved invaluable.

"Oh, you're near me. My husband and I live at 35 Wilton Crescent just around the corner from you. My husband has Alzheimer's. We moved up here from England about two years ago now, just after Matt was diagnosed so we could be near our daughter."

Rachel smiled and nodded, "Oh wow, that must have been a big change for you?"

"Yes, it was, but we're settled now and it is good having my daughter and grandchildren close by. It helps give me life beyond caring for Matt. So, who do you care for?" Penny continued.

"Oh, my husband John. Actually, he has dementia. We have lived here for twenty years. John's diagnosis was confirmed a while back and so far, I've coped fine. He hasn't really wanted other folk involved. He likes me to be the one to help and support him, and I'm fine with that. After all that's what we wives sign up for isn't it? He isn't too bad and he now has medication which helps, so all in all we're doing just fine."

Rachel smiled tentatively starting to feel rather overwhelmed. She realised Penny wasn't being nosey or interfering, but this was the first time she had actually spoken to anyone about John in this way. She was actually admitting for the first time to someone outside that her husband had dementia and this was something that wasn't going to go away any time soon. It wasn't a matter of giving him a course of antibiotics and all would be well. The relief Rachel felt was amazing and yet she was also aware that everyone had stopped and was listening to her.

"Oh, I'm so sorry." Penny understood and could read between the words and faint smile that Rachel was not coping and hadn't really come to terms with what was going on.

Penny smiled back at Rachel. 'If only I could tell you how much I understand and recognise your pain and turmoil. No matter what everyone tells you, the pain doesn't go away, but when you're able to face what's happening, you find the strength to carry on and survive.' Penny was fully aware this was not the time or place to say all that and so asked nonchalantly

"Do you have any children?"

"No. It's just John and me."

Rachel smiled weakly whilst a nagging ache that she thought she had dealt with years before rose up inside and reminded her she was alone and that it was her own doing - her punishment for what she had done a lifetime ago. She suppressed the ache, raised her eyes and looked at Penny.

"No, we weren't fortunate enough to have children, but John and I have had many happy years together which have been wonderful. Different choices I guess." With that, she looked away and smiled at the group in general, her mask firmly back in place.

During the morning, Louise had announced that those involved in the book club would stay on at the end of the morning to discuss the book they had just finished. She had handed a copy to Rachel and said,

"I know you might not be able to stay for the book club, but if you want to borrow the book we've just read you are welcome. Just bring it back when you have finished. I can arrange for the return date to be extended, that's no problem."

Jackie exclaimed, "Oh, it's really scary but I couldn't put it down. I just made sure I read it through the day when it was light and I could have music on in the background. How can people write like that and think these things up? It amazes me; it really does."

Picking up the book and placing it in her bag, Rachel wasn't sure whether she would ever read it but didn't want to appear rude.

Time passed too quickly, and before Rachel realised it people were putting on their coats, gathering up their bags and heading off back to their caring duties. Those in the book club moved over to a smaller table in the corner chatting away about the book. She wanted to jump up and stop the clock, grab everyone and beg them to stay just a bit longer. She wasn't ready to go back to John. Not yet at any rate. She didn't want to go back to the constant confusion and the repetitious world. Surely neither did any of these people want to go back to their own circumstances. But no, everyone drifted away. Putting on a brave face, Rachel gathered herself together and said goodbye to Louise.

"Oh Rachel, are you in a rush? I just wanted to ask if you enjoyed it today?"

"Oh yes, it was lovely. I'm so glad I came. Thank you, but I do need to get back, so if you don't mind I'll be off."

"Of course, no problem. Perhaps I can give you a call in a couple of days and arrange to pop in to see you for a chat?"

"Oh, er, yes, em, I'm sure that would be OK. I need to check what appointments John has and all that, but I think that'll be fine."

Louise realised that Rachel had had enough and needed to get home.

"That's fine. No pressure. Hopefully you will come back next week. They really are a nice bunch of folk and you'll soon fit in. Hope you manage to read the book, but if not, don't worry. Everyone gets to choose a book from a genre they enjoy so the choices vary widely." With that they parted.

Rachel walked along to the bus stop, hoping that none of the group would be waiting for a bus, especially Penny. She seemed very nice, but Rachel was not ready to talk about herself or John in any great detail. It wasn't that she hadn't liked everyone, in fact she had been made to feel very welcome. It was just that she hadn't been used to mixing with people for so long and she needed some time-out before she went back to John.

On the bus, she sat staring out of the window. Oh dear. How am I going to put off Louise from coming around? She's a lovely person and she means well, but I'm not sure she can help me. But then if she doesn't come around I can hardly turn up at the Pop-In next week, and it could get very complicated. And what about that other lady, Penny? I hope she doesn't take it in her head to come and visit us. That's all I would need. Rachel's head was spinning. She felt terrible. Everyone had been so kind and here was she thinking up every way she could to make sure no-one could get into her life. On the other hand, she was so lonely, confused and desperate for help. Pull yourself together, girl. As she continued gazing out the window she played over the different conversations and stories that folk had shared and slowly she started to calm down. The bus stopped at the traffic lights and this drew Rachel back into the present and picking out the book from her bag she read the back cover. 'Mm, not sure I'll read this. This is not my kind of book.' Yet, as she opened it and started to read the pages she became absorbed in the story.

Small seeds were sown in her mind that would change her life from here on.

Chapter 4

Suddenly aware of some commotion and being poked in the side by shopping bags, Rachel glanced up and realised she had missed her stop. She jumped up, stuffed the book in her bag and rushed to get off the bus before it pulled away again.

At first, she was cross with herself that she hadn't noticed but then as she stood on the pavement ready to walk back along the road towards home, she turned her face to the sky to see patches of blue seeping through the clouds and the warmth of the sun penetrating through kissing her cheek. A smile started to creep across her face and the smell of the recent rain shower made Rachel feel alive. Oh, I still love autumn. John had told Rachel that his mum had hated autumn, believing it was a time when everything died. Rachel had never understood that. For her the vibrant colours, the smell of bonfires, crunchy leaves and long walks across cliffs all summed up autumn to her. They had always gone on holiday in the autumn college break where they walked for miles through forests. Sometimes in the rain they flicked up leaves and just talked and dreamed together. Oh lovely, a walk home now will be just what I need to calm me and prepare me for returning to John. She didn't despise John or resent caring for him. She just hated that this cruel disease had taken him from her leaving her to care for someone who looked familiar but behaved like a stranger.

A young mum with a toddler passed. The lad wearing shiny new green wellies, stamped in any and every small puddle he could find, giving out high squeals of laughter. Rachel heard the young mum

"Duncan, watch what you're doing. Mind the nice lady."

Rachel turned her attention to the mum and smiled. She wanted to say; Don't worry it's fine. It's so lovely to see him full of fun enjoying the simple pleasures of life and finding excitement in them. She also heard the voice in her head screaming out, 'enjoy it while you can 'cos it won't last', but she said nothing, smiled and carried on walking homeward.

As quick as a flash a memory so long forgotten came rushing into her mind. It was a late autumn evening and a young couple, so much in love, were walking through the streets in the rain. As they laughed and danced on the pavement they talked about their dreams and hopes. He sang to her "Singing in the rain" tap dancing in the puddles as he went. She skipped, flicking the puddles with her feet, jumping from side to side to miss frogs that had joined in the dance. Soaked through but happy they stood in the deserted street, his arms wrapped around her tightly and his voice gentle yet strong, still echoed in her head; My darling, I will always love you. Together we'll live life to the full and always be together, nothing will tear us apart. Rachel suddenly pulled herself up sharp. She looked down and there in front of her was a puddle. She could vaguely see her reflection and the young girl she had once been now no longer even a blur. A pain stabbed her, the strong passionate voice slipped away and John's voice now so gruff replaced the other. Why after all these years did that haunting voice return so clearly, so easily; yet she had to deliberately make her mind recall John's voice and the promises he had made to her. It was John who had rescued her, loved her unconditionally and given her back her life. His promises had been true. He had as far as was possible kept each one right up until this horrid illness had infested their relationship. She knew in her heart, in the very core of her being that he meant them and she was sure if this awful disease had not invaded their lives the promises would still be true. Yet his gentle voice seemed to get more faint every day that passed.

She raised herself to her full height, stepped round the puddle and resolved in her heart not to dwell on all this or any other earlier memory. It didn't help her and she couldn't cope with the pain. Both the accusing voice and John's promises were from another life now, she had to stay in the present and live for today in this life.

As she walked past the old Victorian buildings, she found herself wondering about the people who had lived in these beautiful solid houses. *I wonder what stories these walls would tell if they could talk. I wonder if others are living a life like mine?*

Rachel arrived at the end of her street. As she walked along the pavement she realised that her head was down: the sun no longer warming her face. She was feeling chilly and her footsteps had slowed right down. She hadn't even noticed whether anyone had passed her. It reminded her of a film she had watched on tv where a man, who was on Death Row, was being walked to the execution chair.

"Stop it," she called out, "don't start coming back to haunt me. As if looking after John wasn't enough. I have moved on and my life and health are fine. I am not the person I was." Rachel reached the front door and quickly pulled out the key, turned the lock and walked in. The smell and warmth of her home welcomed her. She slipped off her coat and walked straight into the lounge where John was sitting, eyes shut and BBC News 24 blaring out. She turned towards the kitchen.

"Hey, it's You, I've missed you."

Rachel turned and saw John smiling, looking at her, his hand held out to her. Her heart melted, and tears sprang in the corner of her eyes as she walked towards him. She slipped her hand in his. The softness of his skin was warm against her and she knelt beside him, looking into his bright blue eyes. His face was gentle, his voice calm and loving. He leaned towards her, kissed the top of her head. A floodgate opened and for the first time in ages she wept openly, drawing herself closer into his chest and lingered there.

***

Louise said her goodbyes to everyone, collected all her stuff and made her way back to the car. The discussion about the book had been interesting, but she made a mental note to ask the librarian for more upbeat, less sinister stories. She mused over the morning, making a mental note of the things she had promised to do and decided she would go straight home and get all the paperwork completed. Her mind went around the table, ticking off the names of those who'd been present that morning. Murray wasn't there. That's strange, that's two weeks on the trot he hasn't been and that's very unlike him. I must call him today. Taking a pen out of her bag she quickly wrote his name in biro on her hand as a reminder.

She had been delighted that the new lady had made it, but even more so that the regulars had made her so welcome. I thought Penny was particularly good with her, Louise mused. *Perhaps they might become friends and hopefully help one another. That would be so good. Oh, I must remember to make that referral to Advocacy,* she silently reminded herself.

Louise walked into the house switching on the kettle as she entered the kitchen. Absentmindedly making the coffee and wandering through to her office she switched on her laptop. Starting through her list she thought, *Rachel, it was good she came today. She seemed very tense and anxious. It's so sad about her husband. Let's hope meeting Penny and Mollie will be a big help to her. I'm convinced there is something else that's not right there but I can't put my finger on it. There is either something she is hiding or something that has happened to her that is causing additional anxiety. I just know it in my gut. I don't know what but there is definitely something. I'll just have to wait and see.* Louise checked her email and set her mind to clearing all the paperwork.

Chapter 5

Francesca left the Pop-In with some of the other girls. They had stopped off for a quick smoke before descending on Weatherspoon's. It had become a sort of a ritual that once a month after the Pop-In, several young mums would get together and have lunch. They all cared for children, some of whom were in transition from school to college or beyond. One thing that tied them closely together was they all had had to fight, (and in many cases continued to fight) for the services and support needed to give their children the best chances and hope for the future. Several were on the autistic spectrum and over the years the mums had ferociously fought with schools, social services and the NHS to get the support required to give their children better opportunities, equal with their contemporaries.

Francesca had been part of this group for some time and was a main-stay. She was full of life and energy, always brightened up the gathering even when she was struggling with school and, from her perspective, their inability to manage her teenage son.

Francesca had been born and grown up in the Highlands. Her dream had always been to get married and have her own house close to her immediate relatives so if and when they needed her she would be there for them. But life hadn't turned out that way. On leaving school Francesca had started work for Historic Scotland. She had loved studying history and had worked hard in her exams. Thus, when she had been successful in securing a job at Fort George, she had been delighted. As one of the youngest guides she was proud of herself and rightly so. Her mum and dad told everyone that Francesca was working out at the barracks, and anyone listening to them would think she was running the barracks along with all the soldiers in it! She loved the order, structure and formality of it all.

The barracks hosted regiments before they went off to fight for their country in the various theatres of war. As a consequence, there were always folk coming and going. Francesca would give school children a tour showing them memorabilia, giving them the opportunity to try on some of the old uniforms whilst at the same time filling their heads with fascinating historical facts and figures. She loved what she did. Being interested in history and people's lives, Francesca would research and find out more and more detail about them, sometimes embellishing the stories as she went along.

At the barracks, there were events that the civilians would be invited to and again, Francesca was always happy to join in and be part of whatever was happening.

She had been seeing one of the soldiers, Corporal Struan Campbell-McLeod, for quite some time. She thought him so handsome. He was tall and dark, with large smoldering eyes which held Francesca's attention the entire time. She was spellbound and she knew it. She tried hard not to let her heart rule her head because she knew he would leave the barracks and probably find another girl in the next place. Yet when they were together he made her believe she was the only girl in his world and bit by bit she was slowly but surely falling in love with him.

On the night before the battalion was due to embark, a party was going on. Francesca and work colleagues had turned up to the dance. The hall was warm and inviting, the atmosphere was electric and the music light and carefree. This was not a night for anyone to be thinking about what tomorrow might bring. This was a night to push all cares aside and just have fun. Francesca danced the whole evening with Struan. No-one else in the room mattered. In fact, Francesca hadn't noticed if anyone else was there.

As the evening wore on Francesca became hot and breathless. Struan took her by the hand and led her outside. They walked in silence along the wall of the fort up towards the chapel where they sat down on the grass verge looking out to sea. It was getting dark with lights beginning to appear across the water giving the scene an almost magical appeal.

Gazing into her eyes, Struan took Francesca in his arms.

"Cesca, I know this is probably a bad time to tell you, with me leaving in the morning, but I love you. These past few months have meant so much to me and I can't imagine life without you."

Francesca trembled under his touch. Her whole body felt electric and her mind confused. She wanted him so much. She had dreamed of being with him night and day and yet she also knew he would be going off to fight and may never come back.

Francesca didn't know if she was ready for that scenario with all its heartache and pain.

As he pressed in closer to her she stopped thinking and with every fibre of her being she gave herself to him.

Struan indeed 'went off to war' and, like so many other young men in such circumstances, did not return. Francesca wrote to him every day giving him news of the Fort and the new battalion of soldiers who had moved in. She finished each letter revealing more about herself and her feelings for him, and over time, about the baby that they were to have. Struan replied, excited about the news of a forthcoming baby, his baby, their baby, and he promised he would look after both of them. When he got home they would marry and be together always. Yet that was not to be. The night Francesca was taken into Raigmore hospital to have her son, Struan was blown to smithereens by a roadside bomb. He stood no chance of survival. He didn't get to meet his son, a beautiful baby boy, who had the same large brown eyes. Francesca called him Campbell after his father.

Francesca did not know about Struan's untimely death for several months, until his best friend returned home and sought her out. She had wondered why she hadn't heard from him but believed and convinced herself it was because he was caught up in the fighting that had intensified in recent months. When Struan's friend broke the news, she was stunned. Her heart was broken and all she kept saying was, "and he never met Campbell. I named him after his dad."

Since having the baby Francesca had played out in her mind conversations with Struan about where they would live, would he leave the army, would she return to work or be a stay-at-home mum. She had dreamed of the pair of them, pushing the pram through the High Street in Inverness showing off their beautiful son. Instead she had been faced with being on her own and having to find somewhere for them both to live. Her parents who had once been so proud of her were now so ashamed. Their beautiful and clever daughter had found herself, first pregnant and now, a single parent without any thought of how she was going to cope with her future.

During the first few years of Campbell's life, Francesca thought things were tough, but looking back she realised that they were easier times than those she faced when Campbell went to school. There were moments when Francesca felt angry with Struan for not being there leaving her to manage on her own. All those appointments to go to get a diagnosis, any diagnosis, something to make sense of the chaos in her life. Of course, none of the professionals would have time to see them in the evening or at weekends. Oh, no! You had to turn up looking like you were a super-parent at nine in the morning if that's what they decided suited them, with no acknowledgement of the effort it took to get a young, potentially disabled child out in a calm enough condition to 'perform' for them.

Her mum offered to accompany her at these appointments, but Francesca was determined to cope on her own. She would always arrive at her parents after each appointment and would tell them everything that happened, but they didn't really understand, or so it seemed, as their eyes would glaze over and her dad would pick up the TV remote, reducing his contribution to the conversation to grunts and nods. She had always wanted to be married and to be a mum, she used to sit in school and imagine what it would be like to walk down the aisle, say 'I do' and live happily ever after.

Always in these daydreams there was a golden child gurgling and laughing and growing into a clever wee thing who was always telling her they loved her. But although she had held this ideal life in her hands briefly, it felt it had all slipped through her fingers and she was in a parallel universe where everything looked normal to strangers around her, but her reality was something entirely different.

The nursery teacher had been the first one to raise concerns when Francesca visited the playgroup. Three-year-old Campbell was sitting on his own in a corner holding a toy truck and spinning the wheels round and round, round and round, without looking at or speaking to any of the other toddlers busily engaged in a riotous game of chase. She remembered how they used to think how clever he was when he started spinning stuff at home and how they marveled at his ability to remember and repeat songs and nursery rhymes word for word at two years old. He knew his alphabet at three and could write his name at four.

Diagnosis had eventually come at five when he was half way through primary one but the school had treated him as if he already had his autism badge from the first day. Because of their early support, he thrived. They gave him special little jobs to do when it looked like he needed a break from the class like taking a note to the office (which said, 'Campbell needs a wee break so please thank him and tell him to wait while you take five minutes to write a reply and then send him back to class'). Francesca had been so embarrassed that he was still in nappies when he first went to school, but so many of the children were having 'accidents' in that first six months, that some of the mums said they envied her!

The real challenges were when he got up to about primary three and homework started. The tears they had both shed trying to get homework done when Francesca didn't know what the teacher had asked him to do and he couldn't remember but insisted it had to be right and it had to be in for the next morning. She often went to the school with ideas and systems to try to make things easier for him and therefore for herself and the teachers too. This reinforced the good relationship with the school, but as soon as one issue was resolved, there would be little peace before something else cropped up. Then when he was about ten, the 'street smart' kids in the class worked out how to wind him up and 'push his buttons' to make him have a real meltdown in public, or to make him do something he really shouldn't. His gullibility was something that would always be a worry for her, she was certain of that. It was just as he got older, the stakes got higher. One of Francesca's greatest fears was that one day he would steal something or hurt someone on command just to keep his 'friends' happy. She constantly tried not to worry her life away about a future that may never happen, but it was like a shadow that followed them around and threatened their hard-won status quo. How would she cope if it all unraveled?

Francesca was an avid reader and a loyal member of the book club. She loved reading true life stories and murder mysteries. In fact, she saw herself as a bit of a sleuth. She was always on the lookout for a good story and where there wasn't one she would make one up often relaying the details to the folk at the Pop-In capturing everyone's attention and making them laugh. Francesca spoke to everyone in the group and actively sought out new folk chatting to them and making sure they were part of the conversation. She was particularly kind to the older folk or those who found it hard to fight for themselves, getting them what she believed they were entitled to.

On meeting Rachel, Francesca's initial thought had been that she was a sweet lady. She felt sorry for Rachel because she seemed vulnerable and alone. However, over time Francesca had watched her and was more and more convinced that there was something suspicious about her.

Chapter 6

A few weeks had passed and Rachel had been attending the Pop-In regularly. She enjoyed the company and the time to sit, talk and listen to conversation about ordinary everyday things rather than the repetitive merry-go-round of the same old sentences time and time again. It took time for Rachel to respond to people when they called her name, she hadn't realised 'till Murray had spoken to her how much she had become accustomed to responding to "You". Rachel arrived just as Margaret was opening up the cafe. It was a cold dull day. The weatherman had said snow was on its way and there was talk about a possible white Christmas. *I think the weatherman might be right, it feels like it could snow*, she thought and rushed into the warm. As always, the newly banked fire was building up and the smell of freshly baked scones filled the room. Mollie was already in situ and she smiled welcoming Rachel as she walked in. Rachel liked Mollie because she was never intrusive, always appeared calm and content, yet all the while Rachel knew she had her own struggles with her son. Peeling off her coat, Rachel sat down opposite Mollie, unwinding her long heather coloured woolen scarf that seemed to stretch for miles.

"That's a lovely scarf you have there, Rachel. Did you knit it yourself?"

"Oh, thanks. Yes, I did. It gives me something to do when I'm sitting with John in the evenings. It was something Louise suggested when we completed that Carer Support Plan thing. She asked me if I had any hobbies and I told her I used to enjoy knitting. So, I decided to get back into it and this was the first thing I made knowing I could use it at this time of year." Rachel folded it and dropped it onto the table.

"It's lovely and I bet it's very warm." Mollie reached over and felt it.

"Lovely wool. So, what are you doing now?"

"Oh, I'm trying to knit John a pair of socks for Christmas. I thought with him sitting about a lot it would help keep him warm and give me something to do at the same time."

"That's a lovely idea. I used to knit socks for my husband, many years ago now. He was in the navy and when we were first married I'd knit a pair and send them out to the ship. I'm not sure he ever wore them, but he told me he loved getting them. I tried knitting some for my boys but they could never be persuaded to wear them. So, I stopped." Mollie chuckled.

"You should try and get along to the craft group that LifeLine runs. It's very good I hear and they seem to try out all sorts of crafts. Ask Jackie about it when she comes in. She used to knit a lot."

"Do you go to the craft group Mollie?"

"No, 'fraid not. I'm involved in lots of things at the moment and my number one priority is anything to do with autism. You see, when my son was young I knew there was something wrong, but I kept being labelled as a fussy mother. He had a learning disability but I knew there was something more. It was such a frustrating time, so when we finally got the diagnosis I was so relieved because it meant I could read up about the condition and then channel my energy into getting the best support for him. I'm glad to say after all these years, my dreams have come to fruition. He is in a residential home and very happy. He has his own studio flat where he can have peace and quiet when he wants it, but still socialise if he so wishes."

"Do you still see him?"

"Oh yes. We meet in town or he comes to me. It works really well. We can have a happy relationship, but he still has his independence. It also gives me peace of mind knowing that he's well cared for because, let's face it, I'm not getting any younger and I need to know he's safe and will be settled if something happens to me. I don't want to leave that burden to my other son, that wouldn't be fair."

"That's amazing. You seem so calm and have everything just right."

Mollie laughed, "Oh don't be fooled my dear. I've had my personal battles and heartaches. When we were faced with the diagnosis we took up the challenge to get the best possible support for our son. But that didn't happen overnight. It took a long time and fierce arguments with everyone under the sun, but it's been worth it. It is one reason why I'm so loyal to this Pop-In. This is where I get my own support. It's great being able to meet, chat about the good and bad times or just talk about things of general interest."

Rachel smiled. 'I wish I could talk to Mollie forever: she makes me feel so rested.' "No Annabel or Louise today?" Rachel enquired.

"No, Annabel has gone to get treatment to see if it will help give her any pain relief. Not sure what's happened to Louise. She said she was going to be here today, perhaps she's been held up in traffic. How's your husband doing?" Mollie asked cautiously.

Mollie was aware that Rachel was struggling and sensed that things weren't all that they should be. She had heard Francesca and Caroline talking about Rachel and although she didn't go along with their thinking, she was sure Rachel was hiding something.

Rachel hesitated. She felt comfortable talking with Mollie and wanted to talk freely with her. But she was also aware that she could easily give away too much information. I must be careful in what I say. Don't say too much, Rachel chided herself under her breath.

"Not too bad thanks. He can be unpredictable at times and I find the constant repetition quite hard to cope with, especially when I'm tired."

"Yes, the on-going broken nights' sleep is the worst isn't it? You don't get a chance to make up for lost sleep and then facing the long days can be very difficult. I found that for myself when I cared for my husband. At that time my son was at home too. I remember one day, having been up through the night with my husband, changing him and the bedding, then getting up and giving my son his breakfast and seeing him off to the Day Centre."

"When he came home I remember sitting down with him discussing his day when I realised I was so tired I wasn't making any sense at all."

"You cared for your husband as well? You're really amazing. I don't think I could cope caring for more than one person at a time. I find it all too much as it is. I feel so helpless as if it's all my fault." Rachel blurted out.

She stopped herself. She had said too much. At that moment, the door swung open and in walked Francesca, full of life.

"Hi there. How are we this morning then? What's new?"

Francesca walked up and thumped her bag down next to Mollie. *Oh, this could be interesting,* thought Francesca. *A golden opportunity for me to find out about the lovely Rachel! The Rachel who some would say butter wouldn't melt in her mouth, but I think otherwise and I am going to find out everything there is to know.* All the time Francesca was talking to herself her eyes and fixed smile were set on Rachel.

Francesca took off her coat. Margaret came over to start taking orders for tea and coffee. Mollie turned and spoke to Francesca. Rachel began to feel stressed. Not only had she said too much to Mollie, but she was now going to have to speak to Francesca whom she had never really liked, believing that was because Francesca had made it clear she didn't like Rachel.

"Well I've had a good morning so far. Campbell went off to school OK and so I'm hoping he will manage to stay the day. I told the school to contact me if there is a problem, so I had better keep my phone on the table, just in case."

"So, Rachel how are you doing?" Francesca plunged in. "I haven't really managed to talk to you much since you joined. Who is it you care for? Oh hear, listen to me firing questions at you like that. It's just I haven't managed to get to know you at all, and all the guys here will tell you, I like to know what's going on. Just good old curiosity. Isn't that right Mollie?" Francesca smiled, eyebrows raised and waited for Rachel to answer.

"My husband John," she replied rather nervously.

"Oh, so what's wrong with him?"

"He has dementia".

"Has he been diagnosed long? Do you get support? What family do you have?"

Rachel felt bombarded and thought Francesca would make a good social worker. "Oh, he hasn't been well for a while, but he has been doing fine" she blurted out. "Louise has been helping me get support from social services so I'm hoping that will all start to come together. And no, we don't have any family, just the two of us, which is fine." Rachel quickly interjected in an attempt to stifle any further questions. She smiled a weak, timid smile and was relieved to see Margaret arrive with the tea and scones.

"Here you are, ladies, just what you need on this chilly day. They said this morning we might be getting snow by the end of the week. That'll be nice, won't it? We need a bit of snow to make it feel like Christmas is on its way, don't we?" she laughed and wandered off back to the kitchen.

The door opened and others piled in, chatting away. The young mums joined Francesca. Penny came and sat on the other side of Rachel.

Rachel was beginning to feel trapped when Louise charged through the door.

"Hey ladies have I got news for you. How do you fancy arranging a trip to the theatre to see the pantomime in January, after all the Christmas festivities? We could go to an afternoon matinee. It could be great fun and if you want to bring your family with you that's fine. We can all help each other and it could be a real laugh. What do you think?"

"The pantomime? You're joking?" Francesca replied, turning away from Rachel. "No. I'm not," said Louise impatiently. "I was just talking to Murray yesterday and he suggested it would be nice for carers to do something socially outside of the Pop-In, and it was he who suggested the panto."

"Oh, I see," said Francesca. "Well I'm sure I could be persuaded". She paused. "OK, I'm up for it," and laughed. "Campbell probably won't want to go but I'm up for a laugh."

"Well that took a lot of persuasion," Louise remarked.

Everyone laughed and chatter started among the group about who had been to a pantomime.

"How about you Rachel? You going to come? Perhaps your husband might like to come with you?" Francesca probed.

Francesca was convinced that now Rachel knew Murray was behind the idea Rachel would find a way to be there and she was also convinced Rachel wouldn't be bringing John!

"Err, oh, I'm not sure. Not sure what we'll be doing." She looked pleadingly at Louise for help.

Louise, seeing Rachel's expression, jumped in.

"No worries, it's just an idea. What I suggest is everyone think and talk about it and let me know. If you're keen on the idea let me know by next week and I'll organise the tickets."

"Louise, where's Murray anyway? We haven't seen him in ages."

Francesca knew exactly how long. He hadn't been to the Pop-In for two weeks and hadn't said he was going to be away. Something was clearly wrong. Francesca had thought about texting him to see if all was well but had thought better of it.

Whilst waiting for Louise to answer, Francesca had her eyes fixed on Rachel waiting to catch any flicker of a clue as to whether she knew what had happened to Murray. There was nothing. No expression at all. Francesca glanced at Caroline who very slowly shook her head and looked at Francesca intently as if to say. 'Don't go there.'

Louise explained that in fact she had seen Murray and he was fine but had been out of town on family business and hoped to be back next week.

"Family business? What family? I didn't know he had family other than his son Duncan." Francesca pressed Louise.

"Well there you go Francesca, you live and learn, don't you? Murray said to let you all know he's missed you and is looking forward to seeing everyone next week. If you want to know more, I suggest you ask him next week." Louise replied rather abruptly.

"Rachel, how are you? I have some information here for you that I thought might be useful. Why don't we go through it together while you're here? Let's sit over there and I'll tell you all about it." Louise stood up and beckoned Rachel over to a table for two by the window.

Rachel didn't really want any information. However, if it meant getting away from Francesca, it was worth it. So, she eagerly jumped up and made her way over to where Louise had suggested.

Louise had grown to like Rachel and she was concerned for her. Every time she suggested meeting up, Rachel always found a reason why it couldn't happen. Even when they had finally got together to complete the support plan, Rachel insisted the meeting took place in the Co-op café and, as soon as the formalities and questions were asked and answered, Rachel left. There was no small talk.

Louise was delighted that Rachel had kept coming to the Pop-In and she knew that Mollie and Penny had tried to befriend her which was good. However, she was also aware that Francesca and Caroline had not been so outgoing which was unlike them. Louise assumed Francesca's issue was the attention that Murray had been giving to Rachel. After all, until Rachel turned up, Francesca had had the monopoly on Murray. All of that was important to Louise but her instincts told her there was something else that didn't quite ring true but she couldn't put her finger on it. It seemed like Rachel was hiding something. There was nothing she could do but be there, listen, keep an eye on things and see what transpired.

***

Rachel arrived back at the house. On opening the door, she heard Classic FM still playing. The heavy atmosphere encompassed her like a wet blanket. She strolled into the lounge and there sitting in his favourite chair, sat John who was fast asleep. The TV was also on. Tea was spilled on the floor and cake had been squashed into the carpet next to his foot. Rachel stood there looking at him. The man she had immediately fallen in love with. Sadly, now his charm, his quick sense of humour and that dazzling smile were all but gone. She dropped her coat and bag onto the chair next to the door and crossed the room to where John sat. Silently she bent down, picked up the mug and cake remains hoping not to wake him. An overwhelming sense of resentment and fear rose up inside her and she knew if he awoke she would find it hard not to bark back saying something like, 'how could you just sit there when you have dropped your mug and cake leaving it for me to clear up?' As she stood up her hand brushed against his. The warmth of his skin on hers made her feel guilty about her earlier thoughts. He roused and opened his eyes looked at her and said, "What day is it? I could do with a cup of tea. I don't think you have given me a drink today."

Rachel smiled and said,

"I'll put the kettle on," turning her back, she went toward the kitchen.

As she did, Rachel recalled the story in the book Louise had given her. She caught a glimpse of her face in the hall mirror and observed the dark, sinister smile on her lips.

Chapter 7

Murray was up and ready early. He wanted to get Duncan showered, dressed and ready so Murray could then drop him off at the Day Centre and get himself to the Pop-In on time. Mornings were often chaotic. Duncan could be uncooperative which resulted in neither of them getting out. That in itself brought its own tensions.

How did Laura manage I wonder, Murray thought to himself? When it was confirmed that Duncan had learning difficulties it was Laura who had been the strong one. Murray had fallen apart, alternating between outbursts of rage usually vented at Laura and times of deep depression. Laura had always battled on, always cheerful, looking at the positive and believing everything would be all right. Murray walked through to Duncan's room.

"Come on lad. Time to get up. You're off to the Centre today to see your friends. You don't want to miss out on that now do you?"

Duncan stirred and looked round at his dad. He quietly and dutifully got out of bed and followed his dad into the bathroom.

"Me going to the Centre today to see my friends. Got to get dressed." Duncan relayed to his dad.

"Yes, that's right. Clever boy. Now let's get you showered."

Since Duncan turned fifteen, Murray had looked after his personal hygiene, so that the showering and the cleaning of teeth and all that went with it was a mastered art by now.

Breakfast passed uneventfully and all appeared to be well. They got in the car, turned on the radio and drove towards the Centre. Duncan enjoyed being in the car and was happy to look out of the window at everything going by. Murray liked the quiet too because it gave him time to switch off. Laura would often jump in and start talking just as the news was about to begin which drove him to distraction. Now, just as it got to the news, he would find himself waiting for her to say something but that no longer happened of course. The silence was a continuous reminder that Laura was no longer with them. *Where has that time gone, one year, three weeks, four days and two hours since she went. Laura, it seems so much longer.* Murray parked and helped Duncan out and led him into the Centre.

"'Bye Duncan. Have a good time. I'll pick you up later in the afternoon."

Duncan went off without a second's thought and Murray jumped back into the car. *I wonder what he thinks about when he thinks of his mum? He always seemed happy to be with her and she was such a big part of his life. Yet now he never mentions her.* Murray parked the car and walked down to the Pop-In. *I must stop thinking about Laura now and think about my friends at the Pop-In.* Murray had been introduced to the Pop-In by Louise's predecessor and he had found it a lifesaver. Mollie was such a big help to him. She just listened to him ramble on and never judged him. Jackie always had funny stories to tell and she, having her own son with learning difficulties, understood and had given him helpful hints on how to handle some of Duncan's moods. The young girls were great fun and Murray felt he could have a laugh with them, flirting with them a little and basically having some harmless fun. He was particularly fond of Francesca. In some ways, she reminded him of Laura when she was that age: full of life and determination. Always ready to fight a battle to get the support for Duncan or indeed take on a fight for someone else she thought was equally deserving of her support. Francesca was the same and he enjoyed spending time with her. He realised, of course he was much older, but there definitely was a connection between them and he always came away feeling the better for being with her. Louise was lovely and always keen to help. There was no escaping that it was Francesca that drew him to the group. He knew in his heart of hearts it could be nothing more than an innocent flirtation which was really all he wanted. He couldn't imagine anyone taking Laura's place but he was lonely and liked female company and Francesca was young, vibrant, full of fun and he knew she liked him and that made him feel special.

Having said that, the new lady, Rachel, was also intriguing. She was nearer his age that was for sure, and there was something vulnerable about her that made Murray want to take her in his arms and promise to look after her. *It's not that I fancy her, she just seems vulnerable and in need of a bit of TLC* he assured himself. With that he swung around the corner and straight into Rachel.

"Oh, I'm so sorry Rachel, you OK"? His arm had automatically curled round her shoulder while the other hand had clasped her arm to steady them both. He felt Rachel stiffen and he quickly stepped back.

"I hope I didn't hurt you. I was miles away. You know what it's like walking along on your own. Sometimes it's the only chance I get to think."

"Yes, I know what you mean. No don't worry I'm fine. Like you I was miles away and not looking where I was going."

She smiled. What she didn't say was that she had been wondering if he was going to be at the Pop-In today. She had also lain in her bed the night before dreaming of going to the theatre to see the ballet, not the panto, with Murray by her side. Just the two of them. She had always loved ballet but had only been to the theatre once to see it. John had never been one for ballet, but had, on this one occasion, taken her as a special birthday treat. She had come out floating on air, believing it was the most romantic evening ever and so the thought of spending it with Murray just filled her with excitement. She knew it was wrong to think about another man in this way. But the loneliness of each night, and every day having the feeling of no value, of having been loved yet now trapped caring for someone who no longer had the capacity to demonstrate that love, for those dark, solitary moments she couldn't help but dream and search for some comfort. She knew she had frozen when he had put his arm around her. That was not because it repulsed her but rather she had felt her whole being come alive. Emotions that she had suppressed for such a long time had suddenly come to the surface, emotions she had never thought she would have felt for anyone other than John.

She looked up into his face and smiled faintly. He towered over her and gazing into her brown eyes for no more than a second he felt a connection with her. At that moment, he wanted to take her in his arms and never let her go. He wanted to run away with her somewhere safe where they would not have to think about anyone else but themselves and just talk, dream, be together and make love. Instead they walked on. Murray opened the door of the café, stepped back and let Rachel walk in first.

Francesca was sitting with Mollie and Annabel when they reached the table.

"Morning folks." Murray called. "Good to see you guys again. Gazing directly at Francesca, he added "I've missed you all." He noticed that she appeared put out and he wasn't sure why.

Rachel had stepped back behind him and very quietly slipped round the table and sat on the other side of Mollie as far away from Francesca as possible. Murray might not be aware, but it was clear to everyone else, Francesca really liked Murray and she was not for sharing him with anyone. Especially Rachel. And Rachel knew it. No-one took it seriously, just an infatuation but everyone also knew Francesca didn't share!

***

Everyone smiled, said 'hello' and laughed at Murray's jokes. Murray had been embraced by the group, partly because they felt for him having lost Laura and having to take on full responsibility of Duncan by himself, but also because he always brought a brightness with him cheering everyone up.

Francesca was not happy that Murray and Rachel had walked in together. I bet they have been somewhere first for a coffee and chat before coming here, she told herself. That woman is trouble and if she thinks she is going to take Murray away from me, she has another think coming. I won't give him up for her. She swore to herself, turning and looking directly at Murray with a smile she said,

"Hi Murray, how are you? Come here. I've saved you a seat. I want to hear all about where you've been and what you've been up to." She giggled and everyone joined in. "Yes, come on, what's the craic?" Caroline asked. Murray walked round the table and dutifully took his seat next to Francesca. He noticed out of the corner of his eye that Rachel had very quietly slipped in beside Mollie. He had been startled by the emotions that had driven through his body when he had collided with Rachel, and he was sure she'd had similar feelings. He wasn't ready for this, it was all so confusing. He slumped into the chair and let Francesca in her usual gregarious way start asking him questions, while Margaret brought over his coffee and a slice of carrot cake.

"Well come on, tell me all the news — how's Duncan? Did you take him to the Centre today? Was he OK? Have you also been shopping this morning? The supermarket has just been refurbished and it's looking really nice. I got some bargains."

'I'm determined to find out if he was with Rachel before coming here. I don't trust her and I won't sit here and let her turn Murray against me — he's mine or nobody's.' She laughed, a bit too enthusiastically but just carried on asking questions and cracking jokes. Soon she and Murray were flirting and laughing the way they always did and everyone accepted it.

Caroline, who had been sitting on the other side of Francesca had not stopped watching Rachel. She and Francesca had spent several hours talking about Rachel trying to figure out whether she was genuine or not. Francesca was convinced that she was a murderer or fraudster. Caroline was not so sure about that, but she suspected there was more to Rachel than met the eye and, as she had watched her today, she was convinced that Rachel had feelings for Murray. Caroline wasn't sure the feelings were reciprocated. After all, he had always seemed keen on Francesca and nothing had happened today to dispel that idea.

Francesca was feeling smug, she had captured Murray and he was obviously happy chatting to her. Every so often Francesca glanced down the table to see Rachel sitting quietly, her head bowed or just listening to the others talking and laughing.

***

Louise had just left home for the Pop-In when she received a call from the office asking her to make contact with Emily Harlow. She had phoned the helpline apparently quite distressed and needed a one-to-one visit as soon as possible. Louise recognised the address as a road she passed on the way to town and so she called Emily to make an appointment.

"Hello. Is that Emily?"

"Yes, it is. Who's that speaking?" she replied.

"It's Louise Sinclair from LifeLine. I believe you called our office and it's been suggested I contact you to see if I can help you at all?"

"How lovely of you to call so soon. I would be so grateful if I could talk to you. When would you be able to come round?"

"Well, as it happens, I am quite close to your road and if it's OK, I could be with you in about ten minutes?"

Louise sat holding her breath, fingers crossed hoping. Please, please say 'yes.' It would make my day go so much easier to visit you now, she whispered inside her head,

"That would be wonderful, so you have my address?"

"Yes, I have Inverforth, 2 Bradley St. See you in ten minutes then."

"I'll put the kettle on." Emily stated. And with that both hung up. Louise quickly texted Mollie and told her to tell the group she would be coming but would be late.

***

Emily poured the tea.

"I'm so grateful you've come to see me. I feel a bit silly now and probably when I explain what's happened you'll agree."

Emily passed the beautiful red and gold china cup and saucer to Louise and offered her some home-made baking, which Louise couldn't resist.

"What a lovely house. Have you lived here long?" Louise asked between sipping tea and biting into the freshly made scone.

"Oh yes, my husband and I moved here over thirty years ago. We moved in when our son started secondary school. We watched him grow up, go off to St Andrews University, get a job and finally, get married and move away.

"David and I thought of moving but we've been very happy here and decided we would stay and grow old together. I nursed David for as long as I could, but in the end, he needed more care than I could give him and he was due to go into a residential home but he died two weeks before he was admitted. David never wanted to go into a home and I promised him that I would care for him. After all that's what you promise on your wedding day isn't it? 'In sickness and in health', you just don't realise what that actually means at the time do you?

"The house seems so empty and I'm finding it difficult to know what to do with my time now. I spent the last couple of years doing everything for him, spending each day caring and most nights I was up with him, so it's all taking a lot of adjustment. I miss him terribly, we knew each other since we were ten years old. We were in school together. I feel so totally lost. The house has so many memories. I feel safe and comfortable here and I feel David's still with me."

Louise noticed that Emily appeared agitated and it was obvious that talking about her husband brought back so many emotions. She was an elegant woman: tall, slim and immaculately dressed. Her hair short and neat; her blue eyes peering through her gold rimmed glasses.

"How long ago was it that David died?" Louise asked tentatively.

"Oh, it was three months, three weeks, two days and four hours ago. Silly isn't it to know in such detail. Most folk say six weeks, but it's not just weeks and days, it's part of me that has died too and I feel that every minute of every day."

"So how can I help?" said Louise. She sat quietly waiting for Emily to continue.

"I'm not sure where to start. You see we only have the one son, Simon. He's a lovely boy and his father and I have always been very proud of him. He is married to Carol and has two children. There they are in that photo frame on the mantelpiece. Lovely children. Anyway, last week Simon came to see me and we were in the kitchen. He was a bit quiet, but I just took that to mean he had been busy or he found it hard so soon after David had died. You see Simon didn't manage to get here before his dad died and that has upset him terribly. Anyway, he then blurted out that he and Carol, that's my daughter-in-law, had been talking and had decided it would be a good time for me to move. He said, now his dad had gone, this house was too big for me.

"I couldn't believe what I was hearing. I handed him a mug of tea, he doesn't drink from my china cups, and sat down at the kitchen table. I said nothing. I couldn't speak and I was afraid that if I did, I would say something I'd regret. I couldn't believe how much anger rose up inside. I've never felt that angry, certainly not at Simon. I sat for a long time. I noticed he was tapping his fingers against the mug and rubbing the back of his neck with his other hand. I realised he was upset, so I started talking randomly about the weather and the garden as I sat and gazed out of the window. I went on 'I love looking out on the garden, imagining your dad pottering around. It makes me feel he is close.'

"'Mum' he started, 'I know it's hard being on your own and having painful reminders about dad everywhere. That's why we feel you'd be better off in a residential home. You'd have company, be a lady of leisure and not feel so lonely. It would be great.'

"I couldn't believe it. I was angry that he thought I should move out of this house but when he said, 'residential home' I saw red. I try to keep active, I attend a local lunch club and a knitting group, and had planned, now I have some time, to go along to a Tai Chi class at the local community centre. The thought of being put in a care home just horrified me. I couldn't find the words to say all that to him so I lifted my cup to my chest, and slowly raised my eyes to Simon's.

"'Remember the day we moved in here? You had just started secondary school. You kept badgering your father to build a tree house. Where has that time gone?'

"Simon laughed and reminded me he never got the tree house and then went on to say what a happy home this had been, and that's why it would be a good time for me to move while I could hold on to those happy memories. Can you believe it? If he'd said he wanted me to consider down-sizing, I'd have understood, but to sell up and go into a home… I just can't believe it. I ended up feeling he thinks I've got dementia - telling me to hold on to my memories while I can. He then confessed that with both his job and the children, he can't always be here when I want him and how neither of us would want the house to end up in disrepair."

"So, what happened then?" Louise interjected.

"I said I'd think about it and got up and made more tea. Simon stayed a little longer and we chatted about all sorts of insignificant things. He realised I was not ready to discuss his idea any further."

"So how do you feel about it all now you have had time to think?" Louise probed gently.

"I know I'm not going into a home and that's final. However, I do understand the house is too big for just me. It's an old-style house and therefore does need to be maintained. I know Simon has a demanding job and his own family to consider, and I don't want to cause any upset with them. But it's all too soon for me."

The conversation continued and it was clear to Louise that although Emily was no longer a carer, she needed support. LifeLine was one place Louise knew could help with that initially and, in time, she could introduce Emily to other groups that could help her rebuild her life.

"I'll tell you what. Why don't I introduce you to one of our volunteer counsellors? She's very nice. She's a qualified bereavement counsellor and she may be able to help you think things through. It doesn't cost you anything other than your time and willingness to meet with her. She may be able to help you in your grief but also in how you feel about moving and deciding what you want. Once you know that, I'm sure you will be able to manage your son."

Emily smiled. "Thank you so much. I feel much better just being able to talk things through with you. I know I'm not a carer any longer but I nursed my husband for such a long time and I just don't remember who I am any more. I feel I'm just a nuisance, nobody needs me."

"You are most certainly not a nuisance. You just need time and support to rediscover who you are. Then you'll find your place in the world once again. You're always welcome to come along to our Pop-In at Chinwags. In the main it is for carers, but I have a feeling you would fit in well, get some support in an informal way, but also be able to help others who are struggling with their own caring role. Give it some thought. Here is a flyer with the details. I'm usually there. In fact, that's where I'm heading now, so if you do drop in I'll be there to meet you and introduce you to the others. They really are a great bunch."

Louise thanked Emily for the tea and made her way back to the car. *How sad,* she mused. *The son is just trying to care for his mum as well as his family and probably deal with his own grief, but it is obvious Emily was certainly not ready for residential care! She needs to find her life again. Let's hope the volunteer counsellor can help,* she thought. *Right I'd better get to the Pop-In.*

***

Louise arrived at Chinwags and Margaret brought over tea and a scone.

"Here you are, my dear, I think you'll enjoy this. A new cinnamon flavoured scone 'cos we are getting into the Christmas spirit," she laughed.

Louise was delighted about the tea but really couldn't face another scone especially at that time of the day. However, she didn't want to offend Margaret - particularly with her new scone recipe! Margaret took all that very seriously. So instead she thanked her and sat down to catch up on the news and eat the scone.

The place was heaving with people. The young mums were there, chatting away, laughing about all sorts, talking about Christmas presents and end-of-school events. Some were delighted that their children were included, while others were upset that theirs had been excluded, as far as they were concerned, because of their unpredictable behaviour.

Others were sitting talking about Christmas and going away to family. Penny had told everyone she was off early to go and watch her granddaughters in their school play and she was so chuffed that the older one was going to play Mary.

Annabel was showing everyone the beautiful crochet table centre pieces she had made, one for her mum and the other for her aunt.

"Annabel, you've done such a beautiful job. I didn't know you could crochet. Doesn't it cause you pain?" Mollie asked.

"Aye it does a wee bit, but I enjoy it and feel it's something I can dae. Josie likes them and my mum sets it on the table on Christmas Day and that makes me feel good," obviously pleased with the praise given to her by the others at the table.

Rachel picked up the crochet carefully and examined the intricacies of the design. She was mesmerised. Francesca and Murray watched her aware that this had triggered memories in Rachel who, for that few seconds, was miles away back in another time. Slowly Rachel put down the crochet. Tears started trickling down her cheeks. She quickly dived into her handbag, grabbed a tissue and wiped her eyes. Annabel turned "Are you OK Rachel, yi dinae have tae greet over this, I can make yi one if yi want," and smiled.

Agitated and tense Rachel jumped in,

"No, no, I'm fine, I think I must have something in my eye. There, I'm fine now. It's beautiful Annabel, such a lot of work."

Time went by. Murray chatted to Francesca winning her round more and more. She asked him where he had been and he explained.

"I had to go to Aberdeen to see my brother. He works off-shore and was home, but he was going off on holiday, so we agreed I'd drive through to him and spend a couple of days before he went off. We had a good time."

"Didn't know you had a brother. Is he older or younger than you?"

Francesca only knew a little about Murray but in her usual style she had conjured up a life story for him and a brother wasn't in it.

"Yes. I have one brother, in fact, he is my twin. He's not married and has no children so Duncan and I are all he has, which means we keep in touch as much as we can. He was a great help to Laura and me when Duncan was first diagnosed. He was off-shore when Laura died. We are good mates. He calls me and we face-time and all that so we're seldom out-of-touch which is great."

Murray carried on explaining that he had taken Duncan with him to Aberdeen and what a good time they had had together.

Francesca was relieved to hear the trip didn't involve another woman because she had convinced herself that must be why he had missed the Pop-In.

Oh, how I love listening to you talk. You have such a soft, deep brown type of voice that just makes my toes curl. She thought to herself. His crystal clear bright blue eyes sparkled and he had the most amazing smile. She loved the fact that when he talked to her he made her feel as though she was the only person in the room and she hadn't felt that way in a very long time. She never thought about the age gap. He was funny, full of life and just amazing.

Murray equally enjoyed talking to Francesca. She would listen, letting him ramble on. She always laughed at his jokes. Her beautiful effervescent laugh resounded around the room. He was interested to know how her son was doing, and they often shared stories.

"I have to tell you I'm delighted with the school at the moment. Not sure how long it will last but I'm happy for now. Campbell is back in school and has managed to stay for three whole days in the first week, and we are now on week three, which is amazing. He has this lovely new learning support teacher who says she's interested in working with me to make sure Campbell is happy and comfortable in school. Not sure if she's just new and over enthusiastic, or genuinely good at her job, but we will see. I'm happy to give her the benefit of the doubt."

Rachel had sat and listened. She didn't say much. Her encounter with Murray when they arrived had unnerved her and then seeing that crochet table-piece had totally unsettled her.

Why is it now when I'm facing everything with John, does my past come back to haunt me? I thought when I walked out of that dark, gloomy terrifying place I would never have to go back. Father Ross assured me that my transgressions had been dealt with and I was free. Free. What does that actually mean? I'm sure I don't know.

She pushed the thoughts away, pressed them down inside again and purposely fixed her 'smiling mask' firmly back in place. Looking over the table at Murray she watched him chat so freely with Francesca.

It was obvious he enjoyed Francesca's company and Rachel thought, *if only Francesca liked me then I could relax and join in the conversation. I'm not trying to take Murray away from her.* However, as things stood she knew she would not be welcome.

She redirected her attention to Penny and Caroline and joined in listening, nodding and smiling at their chit chat until it was time to go.

Francesca pulled herself away from Murray, reluctantly, and went off with the other young mums for their regular lunch. The others started moving off. Louise went round saying goodbye while Murray lingered hoping to catch Rachel.

He came along-side her as she reached the door.

"Err, Rachel, have you got a minute?" She turned and found herself looking straight into his hypnotising eyes.

"Yes sure. What can I do?" she replied.

"Have lunch with me. Anywhere you like. I'll take you anywhere and drop you home so you don't have to worry about buses. I'd just like to sit and chat with you."

"Oh, I'm so sorry, that would be really nice but I can't. You see I need to get back to John. The carer is only there for the time I come here and so she will be waiting to go."

She was in such a state. Not only was she torn because she wanted more than anything to have lunch with Murray and she could hear the pleading in his voice wooing her to accept, but she also knew she had lied to him. There was no carer, she had doped John to keep him asleep while she was out and she knew she needed to get back before the medication wore off and he started wandering around.

"I'm really sorry Murray, I can't." Her head bowed low, her voice so soft, so sad. She sounded so defeated.

She looked up at him again and noticed the disappointment flicker across his handsome face. She felt wretched because she was sure he was trying to be kind.

"No worries," he replied. "How about next week, perhaps you could ask the carer to stay a bit longer? Would next Wednesday be any good? We could go to the lovely little café which overlooks the water and then go for a walk if the weather's nice? I promise to have you home as soon as you need to be back for your husband. Anyway, I need to be home for Duncan so we both understand it could only be a short time, but it would be nice to sit and chat; just spend time relaxing. I promise I won't pry or ask lots of questions and if you don't want to talk that's fine too. I just would like the company and I think it would do you good too."

Her heart skipped a beat,

"Yes of course. If I have notice I'm sure I can sort something out. That would be lovely, thank you,"

And with that she left and went towards home, this time feeling a little lighter.

Murray went off in the other direction. He was confused. Talking to Francesca had been great, comforting and enjoyable but suddenly he had found feelings for Rachel that he had long forgotten. *How can I have feelings for Rachel when I don't really know her, yet here I am thinking about her, wondering what it would be like to hold her in my arms and kiss her. I feel I want to protect her and lavish her with love like I did for Laura. This is crazy. I always said there was only ever one girl for me and that was Laura. Yet I'm so lonely and in need of a woman to love and be loved by.* He laughed to himself. *Great. When I asked her for lunch I thought it was because I was trying to help her. I saw how tormented and frightened she seemed when she was looking at that piece of knitting or crochet or whatever it was, but if I was honest with myself I actually wanted her to come to lunch because I wanted to be near her. This is ridiculous. Pull yourself together man. I've got to get some shopping before I pick up Duncan and then get home and finish the ironing.*

Chapter 8

Rachel arrived home and things were much the same. John was sitting in his chair. She looked at him. 'Oh, I think I might have given him a bit too much this morning. He still looks a bit dozy. I'd better be more careful; on the other hand, if I want to go out next week with Murray, I need to be sure he will be OK. Perhaps I need to talk to Louise and get some help. Or maybe I should get in contact with Alzheimer Scotland. Louise gave me a leaflet about them. Where did I put it? Oh, I don't know –if I do that it means officials intruding and getting involved and I don't think John would like that nor me for that matter.'

Rachel was wandering around the house tidying up, when she stopped in front of the mirror in the hall. 'It won't make it easy for me to get out if I start involving professionals because they will then take over and start intruding. They will see how much of the medication he is taking and that will cause problems for me. For heaven's sake I can't believe I'm having this conversation with myself. I suppose I shouldn't even be thinking about going for lunch with Murray. On the other hand, it would be really nice to have male company and just sit and talk to someone who understands. Funny isn't it

Rachel, there was a time when you took going for the weekly shop to Morrison's and then sitting having a coffee as a Saturday morning routine. It was so ordinary and routine and yet now what you would give for one more Saturday morning to do that.'

Rachel then looked straight into her own eyes and asked herself; "What are you hoping for by going out for lunch with Murray? Will you be content with one lunch and a chat?" She quickly pulled herself up straight. 'Of course, I will. We are talking about two carers, tired from giving ourselves to the people we love. One lunch will give us both a small, one-time pleasure. He needs support and I can listen and encourage him, and he can help me settle back into my duty of caring for John. He's only a friend, so surely there is nothing wrong with spending time with a friend.'

She briskly turned and walked into her bedroom to finish tidying up and then on into the kitchen.

"I've put the kettle on John for a cup of tea, do you fancy one?" she called.

"That would be nice thank you," he replied and flicked the button on the remote pushing it so the sound blared out at top volume.

With the tea made and washing already in the machine, Rachel sat down across from John. He was just staring at the television; there was no sign of any recognition as to what he was watching. Rachel picked up her book and started reading. Why was she reading this rubbish? She had promised herself, and more importantly Father Ross, that she would stay away from anything like this. She knew it was not healthy for her to read it and yet it drew her like a moth to a flame.

***

The crying. "Stop the crying and screaming please."

"I'm sorry, so sorry, I didn't mean it. My fault, my fault."

"No mum it wasn't your fault it was an accident. I left for one minute that was all and just to help you. Please stop the screaming, I can't stand it."

Rachel jumped, totally bewildered. Where was she? What was happening?

"Oi, You, stop the shouting will you, I'm trying to sleep." Suddenly, she was back in reality. Her book was on the floor by her foot.

"I must have fallen asleep. Sorry, John, I was having a bad dream. I think I'll go and freshen up and sort the rest of the washing. Sorry, John."

As she arose from the chair, she was aware her knees were weak, and her hands were shaking. She stumbled as she walked across the room. The old heavy seething sensation pressed down on her.

"I remember this feeling oh so well." she muttered.

She went into the bathroom and splashed her face with cold water. As she raised her head she looked straight at herself in the mirror.

"Who are you kidding? You are still the person you were at 17. A failure, a murderer. You have just been kidding yourself; playing a game all these years and now you are paying the consequences. Face it, you can never run away."

She smirked and said out loud, "And to think you felt guilty about spending an afternoon with Murray, that is innocence itself in comparison to what you have done my dear."

"I have spent more time looking and talking to myself in a mirror these past months than I ever did in a lifetime before."

It hadn't been the book that had stirred up her memories, it was Annabel's crochet. It had taken her back to her home in Ireland. The stunning stone farmhouse which hosted a beautiful mahogany dining room table with, sitting in the middle, a crochet table centre piece, just like the one Annabel had brought in. Flashbacks of a happy, bright, warm room with guests from the local church sitting round talking, laughing and eating were the first thoughts that came, but they didn't linger long. Soon after came images of the same room dark, cold and empty, with the table and the centre piece still in position, but no life, only the strong thick stench of death, pain and sorrow where Rachel had sat when she was trying to escape the continuous onslaught of shouting and screaming. For some reason, no one ever thought to look for her there.

After the counselling she had had with Father Ross, she had found peace and the memories and nightmares had stopped, yet now they were all back again. Was this punishment for doping John, going out and making friends at the Pop-In, or for having dreams and emotions for Murray. It must be one of them. What else could it be? She would have to cancel lunch with Murray and accept she should just stay home and care for John — take her responsibilities as a wife seriously and do her duty.

She set about preparing the tea and busying herself in the kitchen. She went in search of flour in the cupboard and ended up pulling everything out and cleaning the shelves and re-filling it. She smiled to herself. *You are a funny girl you always revert to cleaning and clearing out when you are worried, depressed or feel guilty. I suspect I have the cleanest house on the block!*

John called out, "Hey, You, when is Rachel coming home? I miss my girl. She doesn't seem to be here anymore. Have you taken her place? I don't like it here. Whoever chose this wallpaper and this carpet? It's horrible. My Rachel would never have allowed me to live in a place like this."

Rachel wandered through, standing in the doorway. Everything inside her wanted to scream, 'you picked out the paper and the carpet, you showed it to me and said this would look best and I agreed with you. We made all those decisions and worked together to make our home look so nice. We'd sit down and admire what we'd done, patting ourselves on the back for the great job and saying what an amazing team we were.' But there was no point. "Don't worry John everything is fine; Rachel will be back soon. She's just had to pop out and I'm sure she will spend time with you when she gets back. Would you like to go out for a walk, do a jigsaw or play a game?"

John turned his face away and shut his eyes. Rachel slipped out of the room and back into the kitchen. As she closed the oven door she resolved that she would tell Murray she couldn't go out for lunch, she would tell Louise she wouldn't be coming back to the Pop-In for a while, and she would just settle back into the house. She resolved in her heart to start trying to get John active again and interested in things even if it was a just a jigsaw. They used to love playing card games and doing crosswords together and she had tried to keep that up after his diagnosis but he soon became uninterested and would fight her every time she tried to cajole him into doing something together. In the end she gave up. But no, she would try again in the hope it would help them both live in the situation they found themselves.

***

Murray had finished his shopping, picked up Duncan and gone home excited about the prospects of spending an afternoon with Rachel. He realised that all the way home in the car with Duncan he had been totally distracted dreaming about the conversation he and Rachel would have next Wednesday. He had totally played out in his mind how this rendezvous was going to go with quite a lot of exaggeration! He knew he would have to get his feelings under control but that was fine, he could do that. He was determined to consider her just as a friend and think about how he could help her rather than anything else. But even as he made that decision, he found himself smiling, visualising the contours of her face and thinking about how much he wanted to hold her in his arms. As his fantasy continued, he imagined what it would be like to run away somewhere where neither of them were known and there were no demands or expectations on them.

That night as he lay in bed, sleep did not come easy. He was restless and found his dreams mixed up with Francesca, Laura and Rachel, all of them talking to him and telling him they loved him and asking whom he would choose. Murray couldn't understand how Laura got to be there and how she knew Rachel. And then Francesca started saying how much she loved him and the age difference didn't matter and how Campbell and Duncan could be step-brothers and help each other. Then Louise arrived on the scene asking Murray to arrange an outing for all the carers from the Pop-In and to make sure everyone had someone to sit with!

Chapter 9

Jackie strode into the Pop-In. "Well would you believe it. I'm beside myself with frustration. Louise, I need to ask you, does LifeLine lobby councillors and MPs because if they don't, they should. I can't believe it. I need you to come round and speak to the MPs with me."

Everyone was spellbound. Jackie normally came in, sat down, had her coffee and chatted away calmly. No-one had ever seen her so strident and vocal before.

"Whit's happened to you?" said Annabel. "It's nae like you to be so up-tight, here come on and sit doon and tell us whit's going on." Louise was grateful for Annabel stepping in and she also sat down.

"Well I had the social worker out to see me and she agreed I could have four days respite. I was delighted and I told Jock he would be going on a wee holiday and I would get a chance to get to Glasgow to do some Christmas shopping. I was quite excited, called my friend and agreed to meet up with her, have dinner and then go to a show. However, I thought I'd better check everything was sorted for Jock only to find they had booked a bed for him in Wick.

'Wick! You must be joking. That's 102 miles from Inverness. How's he going to get there?' I said to the social worker. To which she replied, 'Sorry but you'll need to arrange transport. Highland Council's policy is that we don't provide transport.'

"Well I thought I was going to lose it all together. I said as calmly as I could muster, 'and how am I supposed to manage that? My brother is in his seventies, 6ft 5, paralysed and unable to speak, which you know. I'm in my seventies, suffering with osteoporosis, can't drive and have no-one to help me. I couldn't get him on a train and even if I could that means two of my respite days would be swallowed up taking and collecting Jock. Surely you are having a joke?'"

"So whit did she say to that?" Annabel butted in while Jackie caught her breath.

"She just said it was that or nothing. She sort of muttered something about taxis, which I completely ignored. Can you imagine how much that would cost? Apparently, there are no beds in Inverness and that was the best they could do."

Margaret had discreetly slid a coffee and cake onto the table beside Jackie and sneaked away so as not to intrude. Jackie absentmindedly picked up the coffee and then proceeded to eat the cake.

Tears filled Jackie's eyes — after years of frustration and helplessness. She wanted her brother to have a change of scenery and she was also aware she needed a break. She recognised in herself she was short tempered with him and less motivated in doing things with him to help him. She was worn out and all she wanted was four days to herself with the assurance that Jock was being cared for.

Those at the table rallied around her reassuring her that things would work out. At that, the door swung open and Caroline waltzed in, bright and breezy.

"Hiya how are we all today? Hey I've a funny story to tell you that'll make you laugh."

Jackie quickly wiped her eyes and finished eating her cake and drinking her coffee. Everyone smiled and directed their attention to Caroline.

Louise sidled alongside Jackie. "Hey you OK?" she asked.

"Much better now I've got that off my chest, but I just don't know what to do. Can you lobby on my behalf?" Jackie pleaded.

"Jackie this is terrible and yes I'll do what I can but in truth it is more powerful and effective if you, as the carer, tell your story. We can help you with that. Advocacy can support you, but people need to hear from you and see what is happening and how things are affecting you. Why don't you contact the MPs and Councillors and tell them your story? They need to know what's really happening to people. It will also make you feel better. I'll talk to Advocacy and see what we can do to help."

With that Jackie stood up, pulled on her coat and said,

"You know what? I think you're right. That's what I'm off home to do. Look out you guys, Jackie Fraser is on the war path!"

And with that she was out of the door like a whirlwind.

The others chatted away about Jackie's story and various stories came tumbling out. Louise sat quietly for a while, then texted Advocacy to let them know another case may come their way.

'This sort of situation is so unfair. I wish I could just sort everything but I can't, no one person can. Even if I could, I mustn't take away Jackie's voice. She has to be the one to shout. Mmm, I wish I could be a fly on the wall when Jackie meets the Councillors, they won't know what's hit them!'

Chapter 10

Time was passing quickly and Christmas was fast approaching. Shops were already filled with decorations, gifts and the same old inane music blaring out.

Rachel had managed to decline Murray's offer of lunch and had worked hard trying to engage John in different activities; she had even got him to write a couple of Christmas cards. They weren't the neatest and not good enough to send out, but he had achieved it and she had taken them and slipped them in her top drawer as a keep sake.

Over the past few days the chivvying along and enthusiasm about doing simple tasks had worn her out and now she was doing everything on 'automatic pilot'. John had forgotten so was quite happy to sit in his chair and look at the TV screen. Rachel just got through each day. She forced herself to go to the Pop-In and on the whole just sit and listen to all the conversations and contribute only when she had to and then come home again. Her mind, when she allowed it, drifted back to her fantasies about Murray but nothing more.

***

Penny arrived early at the Pop-In. Her daughter had collected Matt and dropped him off at the Day Centre so she could do a little shopping and get to meet her new found friends at Chinwags. She had had a wander around M&S and had managed to purchase a couple of Christmas presents for the granddaughters. She missed her sister. The bond between them had always been strong and although they now lived 400 miles apart, they remained in contact most days of the week. She missed shopping with her and comparing the bargains they had found. Now they only compared how their husbands were deteriorating. How strange that both sisters ended up caring for husbands who had dementia. It might be different types of dementia, but in the end, they had similar problems and the same final journey.

Penny had just settled into a chair next to Mollie when the door opened and in walked Rachel. She had been coming to the Pop-In on a regular basis by now but Penny had not had the opportunity to really chat to her much and she had made up her mind today was the day. Francesca had planted a seed in the mind of several of the regulars, including Penny, that there was something that Rachel was hiding.

"Penny," Francesca had said, "Your husband has dementia, talk to Rachel and find out more about her. She's a dark horse and I think she's hiding something." That seed had been left to grow and now Penny was determined to uncover the mystery.

"Rachel, why don't you come and sit beside me" she said pulling the chair out next to her and giving Rachel a warm, welcoming smile.

Rachel walked round the table and dutifully sat beside Penny. She was a bit nervous of Penny because she didn't want her asking questions about how John coped when she was out. She was nervous that she might work out that she was giving John a bit more medicine than had been prescribed. She had to be on her guard at all times.

"Thanks. It's nice to see you, Penny, how are you getting on?" Rachel jumped in hoping to keep the conversation away from her. But Penny was astute and was on a mission and was not going to be side-tracked by anyone.

"Oh, I'm fine. Matt is at the Day Centre today and my daughter dropped him off, so it gives me a little extra time to myself which is nice. My daughter is a tremendous support to me. She's working but she helps with Matt as much as possible. She knows I like shopping so, she took Matt to the Day Centre to let me mooch around M&S and start some Christmas shopping. My sister lives down in England, which means I need to get her present wrapped and posted in good time. Has your husband got a place at the Day Centre yet?"

"No, I'm waiting for an assessment. Louise has been and carried out the Carer Support Plan — all that's in place. She also contacted Alzheimer Scotland for me and the social workers so hopefully it will all come together. I haven't helped really; I've just plodded on believing I can and should cope. I've always said no when the GP or anyone has offered help. Anyway, I believe there's a waiting list so I have to be patient, which is fine. I guess it all takes time, doesn't it," Rachel responded, shrugging her shoulders trying to sound nonchalant.

What she didn't say was that when the social worker had called to make an appointment, Rachel had postponed it. She didn't want some professional coming to the house in case they found out that she had been doping John. She had found it difficult to stop Louise coming and had managed to arrange meeting at the Co-Op café pretending it would get her out and let her get her shopping. She wasn't convinced Louise bought it but she didn't question her so that was fine.

"How long has your husband been attending the Day Centre?"

"Oh, he's been going there for the past eight months. I must say it made such a difference. He didn't want to go to start with and it was such a hassle cajoling him and getting him there. We used to go by bus and one day we set off in good time, but the bus didn't come. So, I suggested we walk. The centre is about three miles from our house, it was quite a nice day, and Matt has always enjoyed walking. We set off and at first all was well but he started getting agitated and then wouldn't walk with me. He kept slowing down and walking behind me, he was just like a little boy. I kept turning around to see where he was, trying to keep cheerful, chivvying him along, but it was so frustrating. It took ages and I was exhausted. I then made my way down here, stumbled in and fell into a chair. Good old Margaret had noticed me and quickly brought me over a lovely cup of coffee and one of her scones. I just cried. That's why I'm so grateful to LifeLine for organising the Pop-In and to my daughter who has changed her work hours so she can take her dad to the centre for me. It has made such a difference. One day's break I treasure. It's like gold dust."

Their conversation carried on and bit by bit Rachel talked about John and some of the escapades they had encountered.

They laughed, agreed, cried and at one pertinent moment Penny reached out and took Rachel's hand in hers and said,

"Yes, it's very difficult and seems so unfair. There's no shame in acknowledging that. You can't cope with everything. Once you're able to face and accept that for yourself, you'll find the support out there and welcome it. That makes life so much more bearable and helps you find and capture the happy moments that still present themselves even in the darkest times."

Murray walked in and in his usual bright friendly manner made his way down one side and up the other saying hello to everyone before taking his seat next to Francesca. When Francesca was there, he could always rely on getting a seat. She made sure of it. Murray always made everyone feel he was interested in them. As he walked past Penny and Rachel he noticed they were deep in conversation and were holding hands. Part of him wanted to leave them alone realising they were giving each other comfort, but deep within he felt this sudden pang of pain. He could see Rachel was sad and obviously upset and Murray just wanted to take her away from all of this, kiss her and smooth away all the pain.

He suddenly felt angry that her husband was causing her this pain, it seemed so wrong. He sat down next to Francesca and she started laughing and teasing him and he forced himself to squash those horrible feelings. 'How can you be so stupid Murray? It's not Rachel's husband's fault any more than your situation is yours or Laura's fault. It is just what life throws at you. And if you do think it so unfair, why are you not angry about Francesca's situation, or Annabel's, or Mollie's? Get your feelings under control man before you make a fool of yourself.' And with that he turned his attention to Francesca and Caroline. Louise was busy handing out leaflets about the Lifeline Christmas lunch and collecting names for the panto.

"Yes, we're coming to the panto aren't we Murray," Francesca announced as she turned and draped her arm round his shoulder.

"Count me in Louise, and can I reserve a seat for Duncan please? He loves the panto. Laura and I used to take him every year, so I know he'll love to come."

"Oh, how lovely. Perhaps I could persuade Campbell to come too. If I tell him he could help support Duncan, you know how much he likes that and then we can all sit together. What do you think?" nudging Murray while winking at Caroline.

Louise jumped in, "OK I'm just collecting names for the moment. We can decide on seating once we get the tickets."

Louise had noticed that when Murray was talking, he had kept glancing along the table towards Rachel as had Francesca. Louise was not sure what was going on but one thing she was sure of and that was Francesca was not for sharing Murray with anyone and Francesca obviously had an issue with Rachel.

The Pop-In carried on with carers coming and going, sharing stories and drinking tea. Some talked about the latest book issued at the book club and the morning passed by uneventfully. Louise was looking forward to getting the Christmas lunch reservations booked. She loved organising the lunch and making the day fun and special.

Annabel had sorted things out with the JobCentre and she was feeling a bit better in herself. Mollie was the same as always, calm and content, listening to others. Caroline and Francesca were both laughing and flirting with Murray and what was really nice was watching Penny and Rachel chatting away obviously from a place of understanding.

Folk started to leave, the young mums were off to do some Christmas shopping, and others back to their lives of caring. Louise left with Francesca and Caroline chatting away as they went. Murray had deliberately hung back, helping Margaret gather up the dishes. He had to speak to Rachel to arrange when and where he should pick her up for their outing.

Penny and Rachel stood up together, put on their coats and started for the door. They were engrossed in conversation and Murray was beginning to panic. *She's going to go and not speak to me and then I won't be able to arrange tomorrow. This can't happen, I must do something.* He strode across the room and landed behind them.

"Ladies, how are we? I haven't had the chance to chat to either of you today."

The women turned and looked up into his open smiling face.

"Oh, we're fine thanks Murray," Penny responded. We've had a lovely morning getting to know each other a bit better, haven't we Rachel?" turning and looking directly at her.

"Yes, it's been lovely, thank you, Penny," and she bowed her head. Rachel couldn't look at Murray. She was afraid Penny would notice her trembling and start asking questions. Rachel couldn't believe how weak she felt being so close to Murray. He seemed so large, so strong and so warm.

"That's great, now do either or both of you want a lift home? I don't have to pick Duncan up till later this afternoon and I'm making the most of my free time, so I'd be happy to help if I can?" He deliberately looked at Penny because he didn't want to put Rachel under any more strain. He was conscious she was trembling and could feel the heat coming from her.

"Oh, Murray that's very kind, but no I don't need a lift thanks. I plan to go and do a bit more shopping and then make my way to my daughter's. She is going to pick up Matt and bring him back to her house so we can have tea with her and the grandchildren which will be nice. But thanks, I appreciate your thoughtfulness. I'm sure Rachel could do with a lift?" She placed her hand on his arm and turned to Rachel,

"This young man is amazing. He always thinks about everyone else. So, there you are take the offer, it means you won't be left hanging about in the cold waiting for a bus. You're lovely Murray. Now take care and I'll see you both next week" she said and squeezed his arm and then opened the door. "Bye Rachel, take care and remember you can give me a call anytime and if I can help I will, even if it's just for someone to chat to, I'm always happy to chat."

"Thank you, Penny, I'm so grateful". Rachel smiled weakly but with feeling and started through the door herself, Murray close behind.

The chilly air caught her breath and as she turned to face Murray the wind had caused tears to spring in her eyes.

He leaned over her. "Are you OK? I haven't upset you, have I?" He looked so concerned — Rachel's heart melted.

"No, I'm fine it's just the wind and coming out into the cold. I'm fine thank you."

"Let me take you home, please?" He pleaded.

She looked at him and smiled "OK," she whispered.

"We can take the long route if you'd like?" He grinned and together they walked along the road towards the car side by side.

They chatted about everything and nothing both careful not to mention John or their plans for the next day.

Murray opened the car door and held it until Rachel was tucked in. He slid round to the driver's seat and within seconds they were out of the car park and en route for Rachel's house.

"I mean it, if you want we could drive around for a while," looking straight ahead the whole time but taking in her reaction from his peripheral vision.

"No that's fine thank you. I should get back but it was a nice idea. Oh, you need to take next right and I am third on the left, number 7. Thanks for the lift I really appreciate it." She tried to sound casual and yet sincere. She wanted to say, "keep driving, don't stop ever till we are so far away no one can find us." But instead she sat looking straight ahead, fiddling with the strap of her handbag.

Murray slowed down and parked the car outside 7 Blantyre Street. Murray made a mental note of the address, not for any particular reason, just because he wanted to know as much about her as he could without asking or looking as though he was prying.

He turned off the engine and angled his body towards her.

"Rachel, it's been lovely seeing you today. I don't know why you didn't come out to lunch last time I asked and I am not asking you to tell me. But you seem so lost and all I want to do is be there for you if I can to help. Please come out for lunch or just a coffee if that is easier, please."

He so gently touched her hand and as he did an electric current shot through her body and with a huge sigh she found herself totally weak. Murray felt the current too and knew then that their relationship would never be the same. The connection he thought he had with her was real.

Rachel sat for what seemed like eternity and then raising her face toward him she nodded and said in no more than a whisper

"Yes I would love to come for lunch."

"Can you do tomorrow? Would you be able to leave John or get someone to sit with him at such short notice?"

"Yes, don't worry I'll sort something out."

Perhaps we could drive out of Inverness and go for lunch at that new place, The Shielings. It's nice there, fairly quiet, good food and we probably won't bump into anyone we know which might make you feel less nervous."

"I feel guilty leaving John when I come to the Pop-In but to go out for lunch with you, it seems even worse."

"Hey, come on, we are friends, right? I'm just taking you to lunch somewhere we can chat and relax and get a well-deserved break. I'm not asking you to run away with me," and at that he laughed which broke the tension.

"Please come I really want us to be friends," he whispered pleadingly. At that she drew her gaze back from her front door to face him and in the quietest voice said

"Yes, I would love to come and yes, I want us to be friends. I'll be ready for eleven and will meet you at the end of the road, if that is OK with you?"

"Fantastic, that's great. I can pick you up from here if you like?"

"No, I'll meet you at the letterbox at the end of the road."

Murray realised she was not for changing her mind and, careful not to mess things up, he nodded in agreement.

Rachel opened the door and stepped out of the car, thanking him again over her shoulder. "See you tomorrow then."

"Till tomorrow". She closed the door and Murray drove off, his face breaking out into a beaming smile. For the first time in a long time he sang all the way home. He had an hour before he was due to pick up Duncan so he had time to make sure everything was sorted for tomorrow and nothing would stop him having a good day. He kept reminding himself this was just a platonic friendship and he was to be there to support Rachel as a friend and comrade, after all she was still married. However, deep in the recesses of his mind he couldn't help think about them being together in a way that until now neither had known for some time.

Chapter 11

Rachel opened the door and walked in. She closed it carefully, not calling out that she was home because she knew John would be asleep. That was so much the norm these days. As she had entered her home the heaviness returned. Rachel hadn't realised till that moment that the conversation with Penny and the drive home with Murray had dispelled that dark heavy weight. She had become so accustomed to her lot and just accepted this was her life and got on with it. But those few hours of deliverance had reminded her how life had been when she had married John and had come to live in Inverness. The years prior to meeting John had caused so much pain, which she had embraced, because that was her penance. She truly believed she had paid the penalty, but no, it seemed there was no end and she had to learn to accept it and bear it bravely.

Rachel made herself a cup of tea and sat down at the kitchen table and opened the mail that she had absentmindedly picked up when she had come through the door. All of it was junk mail, so she finished her tea, ripped it up and threw it in the recycle bin and busied herself clearing up the mess John had left. She gently woke him.

"John, dear, time for supper. Shall we sit at the table?" She took his hand and led him to the kitchen table where he sat down, turning his gaze towards the window. They ate their meal in silence. John had nothing to say and for a change he didn't argue or question her. Rachel couldn't think of anything to say either.

Rachel cleared up while John returned to his old chair and picked up his book, opened it and sat staring at it. John had always been an avid reader and when they had married, he would read to Rachel a chapter from one of the classics every night before they went to sleep. He loved spending time in a book shop browsing and although he didn't read much now, he always liked a book beside him where he could pick it up and flick through the pages at leisure. Rachel finished tidying up, made them both a cup of tea and went to sit with John in the lounge. The atmosphere in the room was quiet, in fact quite peaceful and both seemed happy to sit in silence in their own little worlds. Rachel found herself flicking through a magazine that she had bought a couple of weeks ago but hadn't had time to look at, and John continued to thumb through his book. As she sat there she found herself thinking about Murray. *What will I wear tomorrow, how much should I tell him about myself?* She lived out in her mind the conversation they would have and rehearsed the words to make sure she didn't give away too much information. Suddenly there was a thump which startled her. She looked up across at John and noticed he was fast asleep and his book had dropped to the floor. She sat gazing at him. 'Oh, my dear John, you look so vulnerable my darling. I shouldn't be going to lunch tomorrow. This isn't right. John, I love you so much please come back to me.' She started to cry, tears rolling down her cheeks and a deep groaning pain from within rose up and burst out of her without warning. The flood gates had opened and there was nothing she could do. The longing to be loved, cherished and to live life again, to feel alive was overwhelming, and as she looked at John, she knew he couldn't meet any of those longings that ran so deep in her.

The groaning subsided and she quickly rummaged up her sleeve for her hanky to dry her eyes. 'I can't cancel Murray at this stage, anyway I don't have his number so I'll go, but keep a tight guard on my emotions and more importantly my tongue; have a nice lunch and tell him this can never happen again.' She rose resolute. This was the way forward. Then she went to fetch John's medication and get things ready for bed.

With John tucked up in bed, Rachel made her way to her room. She picked out a simple cream cashmere jumper and blue jeans, her pearl earrings and necklace — a gift from John for her birthday the first year after they were married. She placed the jewellery on the dressing table, got ready for bed, then jumped in and switched off the light. As she lay in her bed she found herself thinking about Murray but quickly brought her mind back to the present and slowly drifted off to sleep. It was a turbulent night, mixed up dreams of Murray looking like John, her mother appearing screaming at her — 'it's your fault, whatever you do you cause pain to others.' The small voice of the child calling her name, Francesca smiling, pointing the finger shouting, 'I told you she is a murderer. I knew it all along.' She woke up suddenly, drenched in sweat, shaking, relieved it was dark and silent. She dropped back on her bed and just lay still, "Please God help me. I'm going mad."

Morning came, not quick enough, and Rachel dragged herself out of bed and went to wake John.

The morning went well, John was compliant and Rachel busied herself with the housework, preparing food for John and generally keeping her mind busy so she didn't have to analyse what she was doing, or face the guilt that she had pushed down deep inside.

The clock chimed and she knew it was time to give John his medication and for her to make her way to the meeting point. He took it just like a lamb to the slaughter. Rachel had been careful to measure enough to keep him calm and gently sedated so she didn't have to worry while she was out, but not too much to cause him harm. 'It's OK, you're not doing anything wrong, you're not causing him any harm, you're just making sure he will be OK and when you get back you can return to just giving what is prescribed because after you have told Murray this is the first and last assignation, you will settle back into being a devoted wife and care for all John's needs. Forget being a carer and keep foremost in your mind, you are his wife, and being here for John is what you signed up for Rachel and is part of your self-imposed absolution.'

"Right John, I'm off now, just popping out to get a bit of shopping. You OK?" He looked up and smiled.

"Yes, I'm fine thank you. If you see my Rachel please tell her I'm here waiting for her. We're supposed to be going to Glasgow this weekend and I think she must have forgotten."

Rachel smiled, kissed his forehead and turned towards the door. A few days before she had picked up a child's jigsaw from a charity shop hoping that might encourage him to do something other than watch television. She had carefully checked all the pieces were there and had set them all out on a tray. In fact, she had set some of the edging in place, shown it to him and encouraged him to try and do some. Needless to say, as she glanced over her shoulder John had already diverted his attention to the remote control and was fumbling around flicking through the channels. She purposefully made her way towards the front door, picking up her jacket and handbag and as she stepped outside, she allowed herself to think of the day ahead and not what she had left behind.

With every step towards the meeting place she went over and over in her head what she was going to say determined not to cause anyone any more pain. The nightmare that had forced her from sleep remained in her mind, in particular Francesca's, 'told you she is a murderer'. This filled her with panic and fear, and it was about to swamp her when she saw Murray's car sitting waiting for her. She pushed away every thought and just looked steadfastly at the car and walked towards it, her heart beginning to thump and resound in her head.

***

Murray's day after dropping off Rachel had been great. His mood was uplifted and he had found energy he had forgotten he could muster. Having cleaned the house, changed the bedding, made Duncan's favourite tea and even spoken to folk at the centre when he arrived to meet Duncan. Murray felt great, he was suddenly aware of so much around him that he would have sworn hadn't been there before. Even the conversation with Duncan on the way home seemed more positive. I can't believe how different everything is. I feel alive again, I'm not just existing.

Even Duncan seemed in a good mood and had eaten all his tea. During the evening, they had played with his cars and had spent time colouring in and drawing which Murray often found boring, but not that night...

Morning came, but not fast enough for Murray.

"Come on Duncan, let's get you to the centre today. It's going to be a good day, son. Duncan complied, and in the car Murray was aware that his son was watching him. "Everything all right, lad?"

"Dad singing, Dad happy again. Me like it when Dad is happy."

Murray glanced round and noticed Duncan had shifted his gaze out of the window, but he was sure he saw the flicker of a smile on his son's face.

Murray jumped back in the car, knowing Duncan was safely settled in the centre, and made his way to the meeting point. He had thought of nothing but spending these few hours with Rachel. His mind had sketched the profile of her face, recalling her smile and beautiful deep brown eyes. He could hear her voice and could still sense the presence of her body and the warmth that exuded from her when they had found themselves in close proximity. He refused to think about the logistics and morals of this encounter. For these few hours all he wanted was for them both to escape to a place of total abandonment.

He had arrived at the meeting point early. 'Oh, I hope nothing stops her coming today, please, please Rachel don't let me down. I need to see you.'

Passers-by turned the corner of the street and wandered past the car. Each time someone turned into the street, Murray found his heart leap into his mouth, only to drop back down again as quick. He suddenly noticed he was holding onto the steering wheel for grim death and slowly prised his hands off and placed them on his knees.

He started flicking through his iPod. *I should find some suitable music to play in case we can't think of anything to say. I wonder what she likes.*

He was so busy skimming through his playlist he hadn't noticed her creep around the corner.

Ah, that's good, we'll have that because it's gentle and will create a pleasant atmosphere.

He sat up and looked out, his heart jumped and started beating so fast he thought it was going to burst. He wanted to jump out of the car and run to meet her, but knew that was stupid so he sat smiling, watching her.

Mmm she doesn't seem to be as nervous as I thought she would be, she seems to be walking confidently towards me, which is a good sign.

He opened his door and stepped out to meet her.

"Hi, good to see you. Glad you came." He smiled and walked towards the front of the car. His mouth dry, his hands shaking so he dropped them into his pockets.

"Hello, thanks for being here. I'm not sure I should be here, but there you are, here is where I am." And she walked round to the passenger door. He ran to open the door for her, and once she was in her seat, he closed it and slid round and into the driver's seat.

Rachel had clipped on the seat belt, keeping her handbag tightly in her lap and looking straight ahead. Murray started the car, glanced round to see if Rachel was all right and set off.

There was silence, both concentrating on the road ahead, but as the moments passed, the gentle soothing music started to do its work and the tension each held within themselves began to dissipate.

Simultaneously they said, "Everything OK at home?"

"Sorry, go on you start." Murray smiled and nodded at her.

"I was just going to ask if Duncan was OK and check you are all right about this," she stammered. Murray smiled more warmly and gently reached over and placed his hand on hers. "Yes. Duncan is fine, in fact he told me today I was happy and he liked me being happy, so how about that eh! And I am happy being here with you, so I'm fine. My question is how about you? What are you thinking and feeling?"

He removed his hand so he could change gear and turn into the car park of the café he had chosen. He had noticed she was tense and her hand was cold. There had been no response from her toward him and he felt a little deflated inside. He parked the car, switched off the engine and turned to face her.

"Rachel, I don't want to hurt you. I'm not out to cause you any more pain. God knows we have both been through so much and still are toiling on this journey of caring. I just want to be your friend and for both of us to feel support, friendship and comfort. I promise you I will try to constrain my feelings for you if you are truly not interested in me, but please, let's be friends."

Her heart melted, he was so kind and gentle. Oh, how she wanted to be his friend, but she also knew she wanted more, she wanted to be his lover and companion and didn't know whether she could be just a friend. She was torn because she also loved John and had believed, and still believed, in the promises she had made over twenty years ago to love, cherish and keep herself only for him.

"Murray, I'm so sorry. I love being with you and want so much for us to be friends but I'm scared, I'm scared that I can't be just your friend and I know that while John is alive, I can't betray him. I just don't know what to do."

Murray took both her hands in his, "Rachel, let's just take a step at a time. We're not doing anything wrong, having lunch together as friends. Let's just enjoy the moment and let time take care of the rest. Surely there's nothing wrong in both of us having these moments and sharing a little happiness. I promise I will do my best not to press you any further, but please understand I've discovered feelings for you that I haven't felt for anyone else since Laura. But I respect you enough not to want to hurt or complicate things. So, come on let's go and get a coffee. I tell you the home baking here is something to die for." And at that they both opened their doors and made their way inside.

It was a cosy little place, beautifully decorated for Christmas, with a fire roaring in the centre of the room. It was quite busy, but there was a table for two over in the corner by the window. They slipped past various tables, and the warmth of the fire reached out and grabbed them as they passed. Murray pulled out a chair for Rachel and helped her off with her coat, before sliding in opposite and shrugging off his jacket, pushing it over the back of the chair.

Rachel looked out of the window, across to the hills, taking in the different colours in the trees and grass. Hundreds of Christmas trees lined the hills, every so often giving way to man-made gaps which went the length of the hill. The sun was shining, but very weakly, and the sky was mainly covered in a blanket of white clouds with small patches of light blue peeping through. It was a beautiful day, but certainly the winter truly showing through.

"Hello, can I get you a drink while I leave you the menu to have a look at?"

Rachel turned to see this beautiful young woman standing with two menus in hand. She was so young and really attractive, smiling at them both.

Mmm I wonder if she realises this is a secret rendezvous? Rachel pondered but quickly brought herself back to the present "Thank you yes, that would be lovely, tea for me please." She smiled at the young waitress and turned her attention to Murray who was busy flicking through the menu.

"Oh, sorry yes a coffee for me please, just a straightforward black coffee. That would be great," and with that the girl left and they both started reading the menu.

"What are you going to have? Do you want a snack or would you like to have a main meal? I'm happy to do whatever you want."

Rachel looked up and studied the Today's Special board hanging on the wall. "Oh, I think I'll have the soup. It'll warm me up and I love butternut squash soup. That'll do me nicely." And with that she closed the menu and placed it on the table.

"Is that all? You can have anything you want. Wouldn't you like a main course? I can vouch that the food here is really good. "

"No that's great. I don't tend to eat much at this time of the day and I love soup. To be honest I'll probably end up having a pudding, because I have a real weakness for puddings and I see they have banoffee pie on the menu which is also a favourite. When John and I used to go out for a meal, I always checked the puddings before I chose the rest of my meal and that always determined whether I had a starter or main course, so that's lovely, thank you. What about you, what are you having? Please don't be influenced by me, you have a main meal if you want one. I honestly don't mind."

She smiled and looked straight into his eyes. The first time since he had met her that day. "Oh, good she is beginning to relax, please let's have a good time," he muttered to himself under his breath.

The young waitress had returned, and they placed their order - one soup, one burger and chips and one banoffee pie.

"Is that all?" The waitress asked as she finished writing the order and gathering up the menus.

"Yes thanks, that's great," Murray replied. With that the waitress disappeared and they returned to incidental chatter.

The food came and they ate and chatted and laughed.

"Hey this is great. I don't normally have burger and chips, I try to keep Duncan's diet healthy so we are good at home, but every so often there is nothing like tucking into a burger and chips. It makes me feel like I'm a naughty school boy!" and with that he delved in. Rachel smiled and as she watched him, she thought *I bet you were a cheeky school boy, that mischievous grin of yours gives you away.*

The atmosphere was warm, relaxed and friendly. The initial tensions and anxiety were almost gone and the afternoon floated by easily.

Murray asked Rachel how she met John, and what brought them to Inverness. He wanted to know all about her but was careful to keep everything easy and relaxed. She smiled and laughed as she talked about John and Murray realised that in the same way he had loved Laura, the depth of love between Rachel and John had been the core of their relationship. What was sad was that whereas he had loved and lost Laura leaving him free to find love again, Rachel had loved and lost the John she had married but was still held by a love for a man she was now simply just caring for. Therefore, the measure and depth of their love was different yet equally strong.

Murray talked about Laura, and Rachel noticed how much pride and love he had for her. Rachel knew she would have liked Laura and had formed a picture in her head as to what Laura must have been like, making her feel by the end of the conversation that she had known her.

Murray had tried asking about Rachel's family and years as a child, but Rachel had managed very carefully to engineer the conversation back to Murray's family and what his childhood had been like.

"Oh! my childhood was great. I've been very lucky really. My parents were just amazing and the friendship between me and my twin brother has always been very strong. To be honest growing up with him meant you didn't really need any other friends. We had each other and that was enough. It was funny really. We would fight and squabble but if mum walked in and asked us what was going on, we would immediately stop, look up and say, 'Nothing, we're fine,' and then as soon as she'd gone, we would carry on bashing each other to bits." He laughed and the pride and love for his brother was so evident.

Unlike Rachel, Murray had had a happy, secure upbringing with lots of love and joy. As he talked on about his twin, Rachel envied that relationship and friendship. She thought of her younger brother, but quickly pushed those thoughts out of her mind.

Don't go there Rachel, don't spoil everything now. If you get upset Murray will press you and you will say too much and he will never understand what happened. Then he too will never be able to forgive you, so shut up, change the subject.

"Hey, fancy another tea or a coffee? You must try one of their homemade mince pies. I tell you they are to die for, come on let's both have one. I promise you, you won't regret it. Anyway, it's nearly Christmas and we can pretend this is our Christmas celebration if you like?"

"Oh, go on then, I do love mince pies. I think I'll have a latte this time, if that's OK?"

"A latte it is," and he called the waitress over and placed the order.

"Excellent choice sir, they are so good. Some customers come a long way just for a coffee and mince pie, amazing eh! Was everything else OK?"

"Yes thanks, it was lovely," Rachel piped up and with that the waitress was gone.

"So, come on tell me, have you got any brothers or sisters? I've told you about my brother. Come on you, spill the beans!"

"Er, yes well, em I mean, I was brought up in very small family. My parents had me and then my younger brother." She stopped, smiled and glanced out of the window. The sky was getting dark and it looked so cold. Now that's a reflection of where I think this conversation is going to go if I'm not careful.

"Oh wow! So does he still live in Ireland or did he follow you to Scotland?" Murray said with a lilt in his voice.

The pies and coffee arrived and unconsciously both Rachel and Murray started eating these amazing pastries.

"No, he died when he was young," Rachel stated rather matter-of-factly. She looked at him with great composure. He saw pain and something else in her eyes, but he was equally aware by the tone in her voice that this conversation was to end.

"Oh, I'm sorry. You don't want to talk about this do you?" Murray stated.

Rachel smiled faintly, and looking into her cup, said, "No I don't if you don't mind, I'd rather not."

"I understand, no worries. Would you like anything else before we head back?"

"No thanks, I'm full. It was really nice, thank you. I see what you mean about the mince pies. I have really enjoyed this afternoon, Murray. Thanks for bringing me here and for your kindness. I really hope we can be friends."

The journey back was relaxed and quiet. They didn't even need the music to help them. They were comfortable in each other's company and it seemed so natural.

As they turned the corner into her street, Rachel wished she could stop the car, get Murray to turn around, and drive and never stop.

Chapter 12

The week had flown by in so many ways. The doorbell chimed and Rachel made her way down the hall to greet the Tesco driver with the monthly shop. She had reverted to on-line shopping after the traumatic trip when John had refused to walk with her and insisted on leading her around the shop while he picked up whatever he fancied and put it in the trolley. The whole experience had left her exhausted, confused, angry and without most of the items she had gone for. She vowed she would never take him again.

She flung open the door "Hi, thanks for this, can you just bring it all into the kitchen for me?"

"No bother. Only one substitute ma'am. Is that OK?" queried the driver laying the first of the crates on the kitchen work surface.

"Great. That's fine. Thanks so much." Rachel started to put everything away.

She had arranged for the order to come early so that John would still be in bed and therefore would not get confused or anxious about the delivery man.

'Isn't it ridiculous? Even planning when to get the shopping delivered must be organised around John, she mused. There is no spontaneity any more. I think that's what I miss most.' She signed for the goods and shut the door, wandered into the kitchen and finished putting the shopping away.

"Time to wake John," she said out loud and flicked the switch of the kettle as she walked past and on into John's room.

"Morning John, how are you feeling today? It looks like it is going to be a glorious day considering. It's been snowing and it's looking very pretty. It reminds me of the first year we were up here. Do you remember all the snow we had that Christmas?" She smiled to herself as she gazed out of the window towards the beautiful majestic hills and mountains.

"Do you remember the walk we had out in the forest playing in the snow, flicking it up and throwing it at each other and when we lay in the snow making snow angels? I remember you taking me in your arms and holding me close, snowflakes resting on your hair. It was such a lovely day."

She giggled. "Oh but I also remember the snow getting into my boots and my feet were freezing. You took off my boots one at a time while I hopped about holding on to you, then you emptied them of the melted snow and rubbed my feet to get some feeling back in them. That didn't work very successfully did it? Then you suggested I jump on your back and that you'd give me a piggy-back to the car, and that didn't work either. We both ended up down in the snow laughing and rolling around."

Rachel glanced over only to find him fast asleep. She walked towards his bed, stood beside him and took his hand in hers. He stirred, opening his eyes. He looked up at her and smiled. "Good morning, my love. How are you today? Have I slept in? Am I late for work?" His voice was gentle, his face warm and loving.

"No, you are in plenty of time, I just thought I'd get you up for a shower and then get breakfast. How does that sound?" Rachel kept her voice light and friendly, smiling as she watched him push back the covers and swing his legs over the bed.

"OK, dear, I'll be ready in ten minutes. Are we having porridge this morning?"

"Would you like porridge?" Rachel asked rather surprised. John had refused to have porridge for the past few days and she had stopped offering it.

"Mmm, yes I think I will. It will keep me going for the morning," he said making his way to the bathroom.

Rachel followed ready to help him into the shower and remind him to use the shower gel, but this day John just did it all by himself.

"I can't believe this. It's just as if he has woken from a dream and walked back into his life. Should I leave him and go and make breakfast, or should I insist that I help him?" she wondered.

John had closed the door behind him. She heard the shower go on, and him starting to sing 'Oh what a beautiful morning.' Rachel couldn't drag herself away from the bathroom door. Part of it was because she was anxious and concerned that he didn't hurt himself, and part of it was because she loved hearing him sing. He had always sung in the shower. It had always been the sign of a good day to come. Could this be the same today? she deliberated.

John came through. He had attempted to get dressed but had got muddled with his shirt buttons, they were all higgledy-piggledy. His bright happy countenance had gone and a confused anxious look had taken its place.

***

"Well you'll never guess what has happened," Jackie announced as she walked along the row of chairs to the empty one at the top of the table. Everyone stopped talking to listen.

"Louise, do you remember telling me to go and speak to my councillors and MP's about Jock's respite being set up in Wick? Well, I took your advice, called them and visited the lot! And you'll never guess, I've received a letter from one of the MSP's. Here, have a look. But even better than that, I got a call to say Jock has been allocated four days respite in one of the homes here in Inverness, so my trip to Glasgow is going ahead. That's great, isn't it? It just shows what can happen if you take things into your own hands. I think we all know I wouldn't have got Jock into Inverness if I hadn't pushed it."

"Oh, that's great, Jackie," said Mollie. "I am glad you're going to get the break, it'll do you good."

"Aye it's about time something good came oot of all this. The trouble is you only get whit you need if yi fight fir it and sometimes yi get tae the point you canae fight any longer," Annabel joined in.

"Well, have I got news for you," announced Francesca as she walked in and over to Caroline, Penny and Mollie.

Francesca sidled up, pulled her chair close to theirs and dropped her voice to a solicitous whisper. She dumped her bag on the table, leaning her elbow on it, covering her mouth so she wouldn't be overheard. She was determined that at some point, the information she had discovered would be shared with all the regulars at the Pop-In, including Murray, but this was not that moment. She first wanted to tell her closest comrades in arms, which was how she thought of them.

Everyone had looked round, and Annabel, Jackie and some of the others had at first strained to hear what she had to say but had soon lost interest and gone back to their own conversations.

"Go on, what's the goss then?" Piped up Caroline, leaning across the table towards Francesca.

"I told you there was something about Rachel that didn't ring true, didn't I? Well I was right! I decided to do a bit of investigation to see what I could find. I tell you doing that family history project has fairly got me going. I am becoming a real Miss Marple in my old age." She chuckled and went on, "Well, I thought I'd put her name in to the ancestry website and see what I could find. I found her marriage certificate and from that, found her maiden name. There were several Rachel MacDowells so it was difficult to get any further without knowing more about her. I remembered her saying to Penny one of the days she was in that she had been born in Ireland, she did, didn't she Penny?"

"Er yes, that's right she did. I didn't catch where, but it was definitely in Northern Ireland that I do remember."

"Well I looked through the different entries and found a family of MacDowell who lived in a village called Killyman, so I thought I must be on the right track. The problem was I couldn't access up-to-date information."

"Oh, why's that?" asked Caroline

"Because you can't get information about people that are alive.

"Anyway, what I did then was look at old newspaper articles. No idea what possessed me, but I did and you will never guess what I found." She drew herself upright, lifting her bag off the table and dropping it on the floor.

"Oh, hang on, got to take my coat off, I'm roasting."

"Forget your coat, tell us what you found out! Come on stop messing about," chided Caroline.

Mollie had gone very quiet. She just listened. She agreed there was something about Rachel that wasn't right, but she liked her and felt sorry for her. Every time she had talked to Rachel, Mollie came away feeling that she was a woman who was lost, but that was all. Mollie had never thought there was anything sinister about her. She had known Francesca a long time and considered that Francesca had a tendency to exaggerate. One thing was for sure, she had always been determined not to like Rachel.

I found an article in the Killyman local rag about how the MacDowell family had lost their son in a terrible accident in the house and there was a photo of the parents and sister, who I think looks just like a much younger Rachel."

"So, what's your point?" probed Penny, who had been silently listening. Although at first Penny had been taken in by Francesca, the day she had sat talking to Rachel, Penny had realised Rachel was in a similar situation to herself and had felt a connection that Francesca wouldn't understand. Penny didn't like the fact that Francesca knew how to find out all this about people, and was very uncomfortable about her sharing it with everyone behind Rachel's back.

"I don't think it was an accident. I think she murdered her brother and that's why she's so sad and acts weird," Francesca announced.

"Oh, don't be so ridiculous," all three-chimed in.

"You can't go around saying things like that, Francesca. How do you make that decision based on a newspaper article that doesn't even mention any reference to unexplained circumstances or whatever? You're really going too far", stated Mollie.

"Don't you think someone would have charged her by now if that was the case?" interjected Penny.

"Or maybe it was her father and she was covering up for him, do you think?" whispered Caroline enthralled with the idea.

"No, her dad was the local minister. My bet is that it was her and it was covered up because of her dad's standing in the community. I'm going to keep digging, see what else I find, and then have a little chat with our Rachel and see what she says."

Margaret had popped back and forward with tea and coffee. She was intrigued to know what all the whispering was about. It all looked so secretive and she liked to be in the know with what was going on. But Francesca had spoken so quietly and the tightly formed huddle made sure no-one could overhear.

Louise had been busy chatting with others in the group and had welcomed a couple of new carers and listened to some of their concerns. So as a result, Louise hadn't taken any notice of the little huddle down the end of the table. But she was suddenly aware of Margaret hanging about, which was very unlike her, and this brought Louise's attention to them.

Generally speaking, the group was very inclusive and she didn't have to break up little cliques or encourage folk to make sure everyone was involved. This discussion perturbed her because it was obvious the conversation was not for everyone's ears, and Francesca seemed very intense and totally absorbed in whatever she was saying.

Louise got up, excused herself from the others, and wandered over.

"Hello there, and how are we all doing this morning," she announced wrapping her arms round the back of Caroline and Francesca's chairs. They flinched and sat up, the conversation stopped dead, and looking a little flustered, Penny piped up, smiling rather weakly.

"Hi Louise, we're fine thanks, how are you? You've got a good turnout this morning haven't you and a couple of new faces, that must be encouraging for you?"

"Yes. It's good. Perhaps I could introduce you guys to them and you could include them in your conversation. Francesca, one of the ladies has a daughter at the same school as Campbell and she is having a bit of hassle. Perhaps you could give her some advice on how you have approached the school and got results?"

"Oh definitely, I'd be very happy to help. We've just been catching up on things. Yeah, I'm sure Caroline and I could help." And with that Francesca shoved Caroline and they both got up and went with Louise round the table to meet the new ladies.

"No Murray again today I see. Did he say why he wouldn't be here today?" Francesca asked Louise. "There's no Rachel either," she sniped. "Do you think they've eloped?" She let out a loud but rather artificial chortle.

Chapter 13

It was the day of the carers' Christmas lunch. Louise, dressed in her special party dress with tinsel draped around her neck, was clutching the expected list of names as she strolled into the restaurant. Festive music blared out as the place filled, with couples, families and all sorts of groups of people, adorned with paper hats and streamers, laughing and tucking into their Christmas dinners. The long table in the centre of the restaurant looked beautiful as Louise quickly counted the chairs to make sure there was enough for everyone who had booked to attend. Just then, Francesca, Caroline and some of the others arrived.

"Hi there, Louise, we're here. Happy Christmas everyone," called out Francesca. As ever Francesca was bright and full of laughter.

"Hello ladies, welcome. This is our table, so pick your seat. You're the first to arrive." Over the next ten minutes the door kept opening and the carers came in and took their seats. There were lots of hugs and squeals of delight as folk met up with others they hadn't seen for some time. This lunch was for all carers in the Inverness area, not just those who regularly attended the Pop-In. It was a fantastic way of bringing people together that would otherwise be easily lost. Louise had sent out invitations to the carers she had spent time with over the year and was delighted when several agreed to come. Even Emily Hadlow had managed to attend. Emily had never made it to the Pop-In, but Louise had kept in touch with her, which Emily had so appreciated. To show her appreciation, Emily agreed to come along. As she walked in, Louise spotted her, elegantly dressed but looking apprehensive. Louise made straight for the door.

"Hello, Emily, lovely to see you. Thank you so much for coming. You look lovely. Come with me and I'll introduce you to Mollie. She's great and I know she'll make you feel welcome."

"Oh, thank you, dear. It is a bit daunting walking into places you haven't been to before on your own. I was never one to socialise that much, I left all that to David. But I am trying to make the effort and you've been so kind to me." They walked over to the table and Louise made her way to where Mollie was sitting.

"Mollie, can I introduce you to Emily Hadlow? Emily this is Mollie. I asked Mollie to save you a seat so here you are, sit here."

"Hello, Emily, lovely to meet you. Yes, please come and sit beside me. I'll enjoy having you to talk to you if we manage to hear anything above all this noise and excitement," she chuckled.

Everyone sat down, ordered their food, and soon the fun and chat started. There was so much laughter, and as Louise sat overseeing everything, she had a real sense of satisfaction. Oh, this makes my job so worthwhile. It's so good to see all these lovely people having the chance to relax and have fun. They've coped with so much this year, and yet they're still standing, it's amazing!

"I hiv tae tell you whit happened to Jock. You know he went inti that hame and seemed quite content when I left, so that was good. It helped me go aff and no worry about him. Well when I went back tae pick him up he was sittin' in the chair in his room waiting fir me. Anyway, would yi believe it, while I wis getting his things from the bathroom, a wee old wifie came into the room and jist climbed into his bed! I came through to carry on packing Jock's case and saw her snuggled in looking very comfortable. Jock wis just sittin' gazing out the windy seemingly totally oblivious to this. I couldnae believe it, so I walked over to the bed and said 'hello' and asked her who she wis. She said her name was Bella. So, I said, 'well Bella I think you're in the wrang room, this is my brother Jock's room.' She sat up and looked ower at Jock, smiled, nodded her heed and lay back down. Jock just waved over at her. Anyway, I said, 'now come on Bella I need to get you back tae your room.' I pulled back the covers and helped her oot of bed. She only had her nightie on and she was so frail. I felt heart sorry for her. So, I took her hand and we went doon the corridor trying to find a room wi' her name on. I knew she must be a resident because there's only one respite bed and Jock had that. She pointed at every room we walked past but none of the names were hers. In fact, most of the ones she pointed at had men's names on them." Everyone roared with laughter and encouragingly cheered Jackie on.

"Anyway, we finally found the room and I got her inside and tucked her up in bed. She had a lovely room with lots of personal things displayed around it. It made me think she's probably been there some time. She wis a lovely old dear. Anyway, I then went back to Jock. He was still sitting where I'd left him quite content. I was just about finished and had got Jock's jacket on, when the door opens and here's Bella again ready to climb into Jock's bed! This time I rang the bell and one of the carers came. 'Hello Bella, up to your tricks again, are we? Come on why don't we go and get dressed and you can come downstairs and get a cup of tea,' the carer said. With that Bella went off with them. I called out 'does she do this sort of thing often, jump into other folks beds?' The carer laughed, 'only the men's' and off she went. It wis so funny. I teased Jock aboot it, but he only smiled and said nothing. I don't think I'll have trouble getting Jock back there another time!"

Mollie jumped in, "Oh I remember that happened to me a few years ago. I was in Raigmore hospital for a few days having a minor op, and during the night there was an old lady who kept trying to get into folk's beds. All you could hear in the dark, was 'No Daisy, this is not your bed, go back to your own!' The nurse would come and take her back but she was no sooner back in her own bed, but out again and into another one. I think she must have been cold and wanted heating up! Anyway, when she tried to get into mine and found there was no room, off she went, taking my slippers with her, poor old soul."

The afternoon passed very happily. Louise thought it was a pity some folk couldn't come. Rachel had been missing for a couple of weeks and Louise had followed her up, but she was kept at bay. Rachel was obviously not wanting Louise or anyone else to get too close.

Louise was pleased to see Murray had come. He too had seemed distracted, but when Francesca got hold of him he soon unwound and appeared to be back to his old self. He was certainly enjoying the banter this afternoon, as was Francesca, who had made sure he sat at the end of the table with her next to him and Caroline across from him, just in case Rachel turned up on the scene and wanted to sit beside him.

Louise had not been aware that on the occasions Murray and Rachel hadn't attended the Pop-In, they had actually met up elsewhere instead. After their first rendezvous, Murray and Rachel had kept in touch by text. Initially it had been a general 'Hi, how are you?' type conversation, but over the few days that followed, the texts had become more and more frequent and more intimate.

The food all eaten, chatter continued and before they knew it, it was time to go. Reluctantly, folk started to say their goodbyes, exchange cards and, with Christmas hats still in place, wandered off back to family and last-minute preparations.

Emily caught Louise on the way out. "Thank you, dear for a lovely afternoon. I have thoroughly enjoyed myself and everyone has made me feel so welcome. I hope you have a lovely Christmas, and I look forward to seeing you in the new year."

"Thank you, Emily, I'm so glad you came. What are you doing over Christmas? Are you going to your son's?" Louise asked.

"Yes, he's picking me up Christmas Eve and taking me back to his. Then he will drop me back home on Boxing Day, which'll be just right. I will enjoy seeing the family but I'll be glad to be back home. I wanted to thank you Louise for putting me in touch with the various folk. The counsellor helped me greatly, as did CAB, and I feel so much more able to start looking ahead, which is so reassuring. I don't feel anywhere near as anxious about talking with Simon. I'm clearer in my mind as to what I want and feel able to explain it in a more balanced way," she chuckled.

"I'm so pleased. Have a lovely time Emily, and Happy New Year." With that Emily disappeared out into the cold air, the sky now already dark and the street lights and shops all aglow as the last-minute shoppers went rushing past.

Louise watched as Emily slipped out of sight. She was truly a beautiful woman, both inside and out and someone Louise was glad she had met.

"'Bye Louise, I'll be off now. Thanks for organising this lovely afternoon. Have a good break and stop worrying about all of us." Mollie smiled as she passed. "Happy Christmas."

"And to you Mollie, thanks for coming" she called out after her.

Louise turned back to the table and joined Murray, Francesca and Caroline who were still laughing and sharing stories.

"Can I join you for a minute?" she said as she drew out the chair next to Caroline.

"Yeah, of course you can, we're just talking about when we were kids and getting ready for Santa coming. Murray is telling us about him and his twin brother."

"Did you believe in Santa when you were a child, Louise?" asked Murray.

"You bet I sure did. I remember someone at school telling me he wasn't real and I was so scared if I said that to my mum, or said I didn't believe, I wouldn't get any presents. So I went on believing for a long time."

Finally, the conversation slowed down and Murray said he had to go. Louise wanted to ask him if he had been in contact with Rachel, but she knew that would get Francesca going and Louise had had enough for one day so she let it pass. Everyone said goodbye, and Louise paid the bill and set off for home.

***

Rachel had gone to bed early the night before last. She had had a difficult day with John. She had finally met with the social worker and the assessment had been completed. It was agreed that John could attend the Day Centre three times a week. This was such good news but all through the discussion, Rachel was tense and worried that the social worker would realise she had been doping him. John had sat calmly and chatted to the woman in his charming way, and by the end of the appointment it was agreed John and Rachel could go and have a look around the centre the following day and he would officially start in the New Year.

By the end of the next day she was shattered, but relieved the meeting had gone well and John would be able to go to the centre. She had got him into bed no bother and then climbed into her own. She had intended reading or just drifting off to sleep but she heard her phone ping. She lifted it and noticed a message had come in from Murray. Don't read it. Just leave it 'till tomorrow and go to sleep, she chided herself. However, the longing to read his text and talk to him was overwhelming.

'Hi, how are you? What are you doing? Can you talk?' Murray began.

'I'm in bed. I've a headache. Perhaps we could chat tomorrow?' went the reply.

'Oh, no, I wish I could be with you to soothe your pain away! You keep tucked up in bed and sleep well. Talk tomorrow. Think of me if you can.'

"Why do you think I have the headache Murray? I can't stop thinking about you," she shouted out and threw the phone across the room, pulling the covers over her head, she tried to force herself to go to sleep.

As she lay there, eyes tightly shut, sleep would not come. Her head was swirling. One minute she was hot and would throw off the quilt, and then she was cold and would drag it back over her. She willed herself to stay under the quilt till she could breathe no more. The thought of submerging into a deep sleep, never to awaken again was so appealing. She had to find peace or she was going to go crazy. 'I wonder if I should call Father Ross and see if he can help', she pondered. I'll call him first thing in the morning, and with that she turned, faced the wall and prayed for sleep to come to her.

The next morning Rachel got out of bed and dragged herself through to the kitchen. She made a cup of tea and raked about in the kitchen drawer to find the book holding all the telephone numbers she and John had gathered over the years.

Her heart began to beat faster. What would she say to Father Ross? Should she tell him about her feelings and friendship with Murray? Would he see though her saying it was platonic and just two individuals who were part of a group who wanted to support each other through such a tough time?

Would he see that in fact, she was falling in love with this man and couldn't stop? No, didn't want to stop.

Shouting interrupted her thoughts. "I'm coming, John, just hold on. I'm making you a cup of tea darling." She left the book on the side, made the tea and took it through to him.

"Morning, darling, did you sleep well? Are you OK today? Looks like it is going to be a wonderful day." Rachel had noticed John's breathing seemed a bit laboured and he was looking rather pale. "Are you feeling OK, John?" she asked. As he replied he started coughing and sneezing.

"I think you'd better stay in bed today and keep warm. Here, drink your tea. I'll go and get your medication and then see how you are." John didn't struggle. He settled back against his pillows and started sipping his tea.

Rachel walked through to get the medication and stumbled on her phone. She picked it up and saw Murray had left another text. She dropped the phone on the chair in the hall and carried on with what she was doing.

When she returned to John, he was asleep and she watched his breathing. It was very laboured. Mmm I wonder if I should call the doctor or wait and see how he is? She decided to give him a while, and just keep an eye on him.

She showered and dressed, made breakfast for herself and busied herself around the house. Her phone pinged again. She ignored it. Throughout the morning she popped in on John. When he woke she would give him a drink and coax him to eat a little. By the afternoon she thought he seemed a bit better and so decided to leave the doctor.

Back in the kitchen, Rachel noticed the book on the side. Picking it up, she found Father Ross' number and dialled it. As she sat waiting, her mind wandered to the first time they had met. Over twenty-five years ago. Mmm he might not be there anymore, he might have retired. She panicked, what will I do then? Please God, let him answer. He's the only person who really knowing me accepts me for who I am. I need help. Please tell me I am not beyond redemption.

That terrible day, she had been in such a bad place and had wandered into the chapel just to find solace. Having been brought up a protestant, she had never been inside a chapel before, never mind spoken to a priest, but she hadn't found a church where she could be sure no-one would recognise her, so this was the next best thing and all she was looking for was a sanctuary, a place of peace. She didn't want to talk to anyone. After all, she was so bad, how could anyone help her?

He answered the phone and as soon as Rachel heard his voice she melted.

"Hello, Father Ross here, can I help you? Hello. Anyone there?"

"Hello, Father, I don't know if you'll remember me, it's Rachel Norris, used to be Rachel MacDowell. I met you years ago and you helped me such a lot." Her voice was faint and shaky. Tears streamed down her face.

"Oh, hello, Rachel, how lovely to hear from you. Now how could I forget that lovely face. How are you doing my dear? How's John? What brings you to calling me today?"

The warmth in his voice melted her even more and she started to sob. "Oh, Father I have done a terrible thing and I don't know what to do or who to turn to. I'm so sorry to bother you but I didn't know who else to turn to. I don't think I'll ever be free of pain. I know it's my fault. I feel so bad," and so she went on. Father Ross listened silently, his heart going out to this lovely woman.

His mind raced back to the day he had found her in the back of the chapel. He had been beavering away preparing for mass when he was suddenly aware of someone crying in a dark recess. He remembered how broken she was.

"Now come-on, dear, tell me what's happened? Has something happened to John?"

Father Ross sat down in his old, squishy leather chair, looking out into the garden and waiting for Rachel to speak. He had counselled Rachel, supported her and watched her crawl out of her darkness and, over time, emerge into the light. He recalled in his mind the dreadful place she had been and yet with love, encouragement and pardon, over time she had found life again. She had developed into a beautiful young woman who sprinkled love and kindness over all whom she met.

John had been the one to cultivate and encourage her to be strong and live life again. Surely nothing had gone wrong with their relationship? He pondered. They seemed so suited.

Rachel had calmed down. "Oh, Father Ross, John has dementia. He was diagnosed a while ago and I have been caring for him."

"I'm so sorry to hear that, Rachel. It must be such a struggle for you? You are getting help with him, aren't you?"

"No, Father, I've been looking after him myself and yes, it has been such a struggle. I've tried to cope and we were doing OK, but I've spoiled everything. It's all my fault and I feel so guilty and I don't know what to do." She broke down once more sobbing into the phone, the pain of her guilt squeezing the life breath out of her.

"I realise his condition is not my fault, and I've tried hard to care for him the best I can. I do love him so much, but it's so hard. It's not John here now, it's a man that looks like him who depends on me caring for him, that's all that is left of us. But, Father that is not what I feel guilty about. I… I have been attending a support group of carers in Inverness. It's been so nice meeting people who have similar burdens to me. We have coffee and a chat and it's just time to be together and forget about the responsibilities we all have. I didn't want to go at first and perhaps, with hindsight, I shouldn't have gone, but I was so lonely and desperate for someone to talk to. Anyway, I met one of the carers, he's really nice. He has a son that he cares for. His wife died about a year ago. He has been very kind to me and, well, I've met him for lunch a couple of times and we text each other. He knows about John and he's always asking after him and checking I'm doing OK. He's such a support and there's nothing between us. We're just friends…"

"So, what's the problem, Rachel? It appears that you're not as totally comfortable with this friendship as you'd hoped I would believe you to be?"

"Father, please forgive me. I think I'm falling in love with Murray. It's not that I don't love John, it's just that John is no longer here and I'm so very lonely."

"My child, I forgive you, but you need to forgive yourself and remove yourself from temptation."

"Do you think I'm being punished for what happened in Ireland?" she whispered.

"No, my child, I don't. We dealt with that when we met all those years ago. The drowning of your brother was not your fault. It was a tragic accident that you could not prevent and was never your responsibility. Until you believe and accept that, you will live in condemnation. Rachel, you must accept that you're only responsible for your actions and for you, at this moment, that is with your commitment to John and your choices concerning the other friendships you form."

"Thank you, Father, but that's not all. For me to be able to go to the Pop-In I…"

"Rachel, are you there?" John shouted out and then started a coughing fit and was obviously finding it hard to breathe.

"Oh, Father, I need to go. John needs me. Sorry to bother you. Thanks for your help. Bye for now." She dropped the phone and ran through to the bedroom.

He was very hot and sweaty and was finding it difficult to breathe. Rachel helped him sit up, puffed up his pillows and settled him back against them. She gave him some water, and then got a cold flannel, placing it on his forehead. He didn't struggle. He gently complied with her instructions and smiled weakly as he closed his eyes and began to drift off to sleep once more.

Rachel busied herself around the house, tidying up the papers and John's books. She put on a load of washing, started cleaning the windows and then tackled the bathroom cupboard. She always cleaned and tidied up when she was stressed. It was just as if it was her way of cleansing herself. She heard her mobile ping several times, but she ignored it. She knew it would be Murray and she couldn't talk to him now. Perhaps she would never speak to him again. She couldn't think about all that now. She just had to keep cleaning and caring for John. Nothing else mattered. Nothing.

Chapter 14

The rest of the day went by in a blur. The house was sparkling and smelling fresh and clean. John had slept most of the time and when he did wake, Rachel dutifully and lovingly helped him in any way she could. She changed the sheets, helped him change his pyjamas and sat for a while holding his hand, silently watching him. His breathing was less laboured and by tea time, his temperature seemed much better.

She couldn't face making a meal for herself, so made some toast and banana and went through to the lounge, switched on the TV and, pre-occupied, ate her meagre meal.

A Christmas Carol was about to start. She just sat staring at the screen. It was one of her favourite films which she had watched a hundred times and so it was easy to simply sit and let it wash over her.

I feel a bit like Scrooge, she thought as she sat watching her past, present and future stare at her. *My brother, my poor little beloved brother. Why did he have to drown? It wasn't his fault that our mother was a drunk who'd relinquished her responsibilities as a mother onto me, a fourteen-year-old girl. If only I hadn't left Daniel in the bath and gone to help mum, who'd fallen again on the stairs because she couldn't see where she was going. He would probably have been alive today.* But even as she thought this, she had a flash of the scene she had replayed over and over again in her mind. Suddenly, she became aware of a voice, a familiar voice, calling up the stairs to mum. 'Who's that? Why don't they come and help? Why has it been left to me?' In a flash, it came to her. The other voice was her father, calling out from the dining room asking everyone to quieten down as he was trying to concentrate on what he was doing. If only he had come to help, he could have helped Daniel, or tended to mum and let me stay with Daniel.

Just as the scene changed on the TV, Rachel was aware of John calling out. She arose and went to him. Everything seemed so surreal. As she entered the room he glanced over and in nothing more than a whisper called her name.

"Rachel, my love, could you get me a drink? I'm so thirsty and so hot."

"Of course, darling. I'll get it and be back in a second. She rushed through to the kitchen, grabbed a glass of water and whisked into the bathroom picking up a flannel which she ran under the cold tap, and was back at his side in seconds.

"Come on, John, let's sit you up so you can drink this more easily." With that she reached round, puffed up his pillows again and helped him sit more upright in the bed. His skin was hot to touch, his pyjama jacket soaked in sweat. She placed the flannel on his brow and while he was sipping the water she went and fetched clean pyjamas for him. She helped him change and snuggle back in bed.

He smiled as he closed his eyes and sunk into the pillows. "Thanks, dear, that feels so much better. Where would I be without you?" He clasped her hand in his and slowly drifted off to sleep. Rachel stood beside him for some time leaving her hand in his. Those few words meant more than the thousands of painful words previously spoken. She stroked his brow and dabbed the flannel over his face and neck and then, when she knew his breathing was steady and he was peaceful, she gathered up everything, switched off the light and quietly crept out of the room.

She was tired and so restless. She dumped everything in the kitchen sink and fell back into the sofa to watch the rest of the film. Scrooge was just leaving his present and about to face his future. Rachel found herself lost in her own present. Those last few moments made her believe she could continue to cope and care for John. She knew her wedding promises 'for better or worse' still meant everything to her and regardless of why all this had happened, she knew that she wanted to continue being John's wife first and foremost, but also his carer.

She knew that the few kind words spoken may never come again and by the time he woke in the morning, she may be back to being called 'You.' But deep down, she knew John her beloved husband, lover and friend, still loved and needed her and she needed him.

As she glanced at the TV where Scrooge was meeting his potential future, Rachel's thoughts went to Murray. She was grateful to have met him and yes, part of her did love him, but not in the way she loved John. Murray had come into her life when she was most vulnerable and when her emotions were both raw and confused. She wanted Murray as a friend, a dear friend, but she was clear in her mind that was all for now. Whether more could ever come of things in the future, no one knew. But for now, at least, friendship was all she was able and willing to give.

As the film came to an end, Rachel got up, switched off the TV, tidied the lounge and went to clear up before she made a last check on John and went to bed.

As she passed the chair in the hall, she noticed her phone lying there. She picked it up and realised the battery had died so she plugged it in and while she was getting ready for bed she could hear loads of messages pinging through.

She picked the phone up and glanced through them. All were from Murray, asking if she was OK, and could they talk? Messages telling Rachel he was missing her and hoped they could meet for a quick coffee and chat tomorrow which was Christmas Eve. She smiled as she placed the phone on the side and climbed into bed. She would wait till tomorrow before messaging him back. Twenty-four hours ago, she wouldn't have been able to resist contacting him, but she was resolute that she would wait till the morning. She needed time to think how she was going to tell him what she was feeling.

She slept peacefully, the best she had slept in weeks, and when she woke the next day her spirit felt so much lighter. She got up and went to see how John was doing. He was still sleeping. He was hot and she decided she would call the doctor as soon as she had got dressed.

She picked up her phone and texted Murray,

'Hi, sorry I haven't been in touch. John has been quite unwell and I've been caught up caring for him. Hope all is well with you. I don't think I'll be able to meet you. John is still not well and I'm waiting for the doctor to call. Hope you have a wonderful time over Christmas. Perhaps we can catch up after the celebrations are over? Hope you enjoy the time with Duncan and your brother. X'

She called the surgery and asked for a house call. The receptionist said Dr Fraser would come as soon as his surgery was over. With that Rachel sat quietly beside John. She just wanted to be near him.

John was very weak and seemed so frail. This episode had taken its toll on him. He was compliant, but the tenderness, lucidity and recognition from the night before had gone.

Her phone rang and she was tempted not to answer it, but she knew that would be unfair on Murray and she didn't want to hurt him either.

"Hello," she began,

"Hey, how are you? I've been worrying about you. You didn't reply to any of my calls or messages yesterday. I miss you when I don't hear from you," Murray spoke gently into the phone.

"Oh, I'm sorry. I've been looking after John. He's not at all well and so I've been busy with him. I also hadn't realised my phone had died on me, sorry. How are you? Everything OK?" she said quite brusquely.

"Yeah, everything's fine with me. Not sure what's going on with you though. Rachel, please tell me what's happened?"

"Nothing, Murray. I've told you. John's not well and I'm caught up caring for him. I'm not only his carer. I'm his wife, remember?"

"Oh, OK. I'm sorry. Is there anything I can do? Duncan is out with my brother doing his Christmas shopping. I could pop round, get you some shopping, anything. Rachel, I want to help you, please don't shut me out. I always said I'm first and foremost your friend and I want to be there for you in any way I can."

"Oh Murray, I'm so sorry." The tears started to roll down her cheeks. She didn't want to hurt him and she needed a friend, but at this moment in time she knew it couldn't be him.

"Thank you, I really appreciate that, but I'm fine. I'm waiting for the doctor to call. Once I know what he says, I'll phone you and I'll probably feel better and more able to chat. Is that OK with you?"

"Yeah, OK, whatever you want. You know where I am. Please don't hesitate to call me if I can help. Bye for now, take care." He seemed so dejected, but she knew she had done the right thing.

The doorbell rang. Dr Fraser had arrived. Rachel went to let him in.

Chapter 15

Murray snapped his phone shut tossing it on the side. 'What is wrong with her. What have I done? We got on so well the other day? I must have said something to upset her. I know her husband isn't well, but it's just as if suddenly I'm a stranger. Oh well there's nothing I can do about it so I just have to wait and see. Duncan and Graeme will be back soon so I better get Duncan's presents wrapped and under the tree.'

Murray went into his wardrobe pulled out the bag of presents he had gathered over the past few weeks and picking up paper and Sellotape en-route, he went into the lounge, switched on his music and busied himself diverting his thoughts to Duncan and Laura.

Laura, I wonder what you would say if you were here. I think you would like Rachel and I know you would have got involved trying to help. Am I wrong to want friendship and companionship now that you've gone? I'm so lonely and tired and I just want a normal life — whatever that is. I just want some fun and freedom, not having to think about someone else all the time because they're dependent on me. I want an equal partnership.

The paper ripped, the Sellotape got stuck on the main piece of paper and there wasn't enough to wrap the shiny new red remote-controlled car. In a temper, Murray scrunched up the paper and threw it across the room and burst into tears.

He sobbed and sobbed for what seemed an age until there were no more tears to cry.

"Oh, for goodness sake, pull yourself together man and get these presents wrapped before Duncan returns," he reprimanded himself.

He switched the music off whilst simultaneously turning the TV on. He didn't care what was on, he just needed voices and some normality and not sentiment.

"The bottom line is, Murray," he said out loud, "if Rachel's going to mess you around or give you more hassle than you already have, then forget her and move on. Your immediate priority is Duncan and making Christmas a happy time for him. Anyway, there's always Francesca. You know if you gave her any hint of interest she'd come running so that's a nice back-up."

He chuckled to himself. In his heart he knew he would never use Francesca, but the thought made him feel at least he wasn't totally past it and someone somewhere might one day walk into his life.

***

Francesca was all ready for Christmas. Campbell had chosen his presents, everything was wrapped, food bought and the house all tidy and beautifully decorated.

Campbell was spending the day with his gran. Francesca had asked her mum to have him so she could get everything ready without any interruptions. She had actually sold it to her mum by saying how much Campbell had gone on about seeing his gran and grandda on Christmas Eve and how much fun it was being with them.

In truth, Campbell had agreed to go, but just because it was something to do and he secretly hoped gran would give him an extra present and some lovely ice-cream and cakes. Francesca needed it to happen because she wanted time to herself.

As she was going through the parcels she noticed a small one sitting on its own. She picked it up. "Oh, this is the one I bought for Murray but I didn't get to give it to him. What a shame. I wonder what he's doing today, perhaps I could give him a call and suggest we meet up for coffee. If I suggested I brought Campbell and he brought Duncan and waffled on about how nice it would be for the boys to see each other before Christmas and the Pantomime, he might buy the idea," she told herself.

She hesitated and thought to herself. *Murray has changed since that Rachel has come on the scene. I can't believe Murray sees anything in her. She's always so miserable and if what I have found out to be true is true, then he shouldn't get mixed up with her.*

'He's so much more suited to me.' She stood with her phone in her hand admiring her new hair-do in the hall mirror. 'Oh! I'm going to give him a call. Shame to have such a nice new hair-cut and no-one to show it off to.'

***

The last parcel was wrapped and the remains of the paper thrown away. Everything was set and Murray had determined in his heart to make sure he, his brother and Duncan had a great time.

As he was switching off the TV, the phone rang. His heart missed a beat. "Could this be Rachel?" he muttered to himself.

He was so keen to answer, he didn't check the name that came up on the screen.

"Hi, how are you? Everything OK?" he blurted out excitedly.

"Oh! Hi, Murray, everything is fine." Francesca jumped, surprised at how enthusiastic he was when he answered. She was also relieved as he obviously wasn't with Rachel. After all, if he was, he wouldn't have sounded so pleased to hear from her, she mused.

"Ah, Francesca, how lovely to hear from you," he continued, trying to get his head round what was going on. He was convinced it would be Rachel calling, so on hearing Francesca's voice it had thrown him.

"What can I do for you?" he went on. "Everything ready for Christmas?"

"Oh yeah, I'm as ready as I will ever be. How about you?"

"Yip, funnily enough if you had called ten minutes ago you would have been greeted with a grumpy frustrated old man. I've been wrapping up presents and got most of the Sellotape around me and parts of the paper that don't need sticking. I hate wrapping gifts. Laura always dealt with that and everything looked so beautiful and mysterious. I think as soon as Duncan sees the parcel he'll know it's a car. Still at least it's wrapped," he chuckled into the phone.

"Aw you put yourself down, Murray. I'm sure it will look great and Duncan will be so pleased with it all. I spend ages wrapping presents and I don't think Campbell even notices. He just dives in and before you know it there is paper everywhere and he is absorbed in whatever was in it."

Both sides went silent.

"What can I do for you Francesca? Was there something you wanted?"

Oh yes, I want you Murray, here beside me with your arms around me promising me you will never let me go. That was what was in her head, but instead she said "Oh, I just wondered if you're all sorted for Christmas and have an hour or so free? How do you fancy meeting for a coffee today? If you want you could bring Duncan and I would get Campbell to come along and they could chat and all that and we could have a laugh and just chill for a bit. No pressure, and I understand if you have too much to do or you have other plans?" She wanted to say, 'plans to meet that wicked woman Rachel.' But she didn't. She stopped and waited, crossing her fingers, squeezing her eyes shut tight and holding her breath.

Murray was about to say 'no', but something inside melted. He wanted a friend, Rachel was obviously not interested and here was Francesca calling and asking him. He liked her company and he knew they would have a laugh and it would cheer him up.

"Oh OK, I tell you what, why don't I drop by and pick you up and take you to a lovely little place outside Inverness? Duncan is out with my brother at the moment and I will call him and tell him that I've popped out for a couple of hours and he will be fine with that. Are you OK to pop out without

Campbell?" It was his time to hold his breath and cross his fingers.

"Yeah, are you sure? I would love that. No, I mean yes. Campbell can go to his gran for a while. That's no problem. Oh, Murray, that will be lovely thanks so much. I really appreciate it. I don't want you to feel under pressure or anything. I was just thinking it would be a bit of fun."

"It would be a pleasure Francesca. See you in about 15 minutes OK?"

"Great! Yes. See you then," and with that they both finished the call.

Murray quickly dialled Graeme's number.

"Whatcha mate, everything OK?"

"Yeah, we've had a great morning. All OK with you?"

"Yeah, I was just wondering. Are you OK to keep Duncan for another couple of hours? I just need to pop out for a bit?"

"Yeah, that's fine. We'll probably go and get something to eat and then come home and wrap our presents, so don't worry. Take whatever time you want."

Murray was relieved, excited and felt like a foolish schoolboy all at the one time.

He picked up his jacket, ran his fingers through his hair as he passed the mirror and went out of the door.

Chapter 16

Francesca couldn't believe it; her Christmas wish had come true. 'I need to change — what shall I wear? Oh, now I'm all in a dither. I know I will keep it simple and casual. It mustn't look like I have dressed up for him.'

She quickly ran upstairs and pulled out her red jumper which went nicely with her black jeans and black padded jacket which all showed off her new hair style perfectly.

She dropped the small present into her bag and sat looking out of the window for his car.

As promised, Murray pulled up outside the door fifteen minutes later and strolled up to her front path.

'I can't believe it. I've wanted this for so long. It feels like a real date.' She grabbed her bag and nonchalantly walked to the door and opened it. 'Now don't spoil it Francesca, don't bring up Rachel, just enjoy yourself.'

"Hey, good timing," Francesca said as she beamed and looked straight into Murray's eyes.

"Oh, now who's had their hair done then? Very nice. It suits you. There you go, in you get, my lady." Murray opened the door and directed her into the car. He scooted round and hopped in and they drove away.

It's so much more relaxed than the time I took Rachel out for the first time, he thought. *Now Murray, stop comparing Rachel with Francesca. You're with Francesca now, she offered to spend time with you. Don't spoil it.*

He turned and glanced at Francesca. She was a beautiful, warm, loving young woman and even with all she had to deal with, she always looked on the bright side of life.

"Hey, Murray, I love your car. Love the colour. I'm going to have to try and change my car next year. It's a right old banger and beginning to get a bit unreliable. Not that I could afford as lovely a car as this, but I need something that will get me by. My dad will probably come and help me choose it; he knows quite a bit about them and of course, Campbell will have a view."

"Yes, cars are a drain on the old finances aren't they? Yet we need them don't we? I love this car. I have had it about two years now and it's just fine."

"So where are you taking me? I didn't mean you to go out of your way. I was happy to meet in town."

"Oh, I know, but then I thought it would be a nice Christmas treat for us both. Anyway, it's nice to go somewhere different isn't it?"

Francesca smiled and gazed out of the window.

"Thank you so much for this Murray. I haven't felt this special in a long time." She blurted out and suddenly felt really embarrassed. "I mean it's so kind of you to meet up with me, my old friend." She thought by emphasising the 'old friend' bit he would think she didn't think of him in any other way.

"Hey! Forget the 'old' bit. It makes me feel like I'm ninety!" he chuckled.

They reached the café and Murray quickly whisked round and held open the door.

"He's such a gentleman. I just love him. Please God, let my dream come true. Let him fall in love with me and I promise I will always be true to him." She whispered under her breath.

They walked in and found a table, right next to the one he had sat at with Rachel. He pushed the thought right out of his mind.

The time passed quickly. The conversation had been easy, light, fun and relaxing. They talked about the boys, and the ups and downs of being a parent and managing on their own. Francesca had wanted to ask about Laura, but decided that might be a step too far and so instead asked about his twin.

"I didn't know you were a twin till the other day. Do you look alike?"

"No. People say we sound alike and have similar mannerisms but I'm the good-looking one." He laughed.

"There's no-one as brilliant as Graeme. He has always been my best friend all through life both in the ups and downs. Laura used to say when we got together no-one else existed. We can talk for hours and it just seems like seconds. Over the past year or so, when Laura was first ill and then died, Graeme was a tremendous support. I don't think I would've survived as well as I have if it wasn't for him. And he is great with Duncan. He plays with him and just interacts on a level that Duncan responds to. He is truly amazing."

"Is he married?"

"No, he was engaged at one point, but she broke his heart and he never found anyone to take her place. Don't get me wrong, he has had several relationships but nothing permanent. It's such a shame because he would have made a brilliant dad. Instead he has thrown himself into his career and has been very successful."

"What about you, have you any brothers or sisters?"

"No, I'm an only child. I always wanted to be a twin or at least have a sister, but it wasn't to be. My mum used to say I should be thankful because it meant I didn't have to share anything and they could simply just spoil me. But I used to envy my best friend who had four sisters. Their house was full of life and laughter and they would chat away and share clothes and all that. It all seemed such fun. Still, that's how it is. My parents have been very good to me. They were there for me when Campbell was born and when I got his diagnosis and even now, I can call on them any time and if they can they will help me. I'm so lucky."

The atmosphere was so welcoming, as if it was clinging on to them to keep them both there as long as possible. It drew the hidden stories out into the open, and both of them would join in with the other, sharing more and more of their personal dreams and hopes.

Murray's phone pinged, propelling him back to reality. At first, he ignored it, but then a nagging thought invaded his mind. Maybe it was Graeme and something was wrong.

"Sorry my phone's just pinged. I better check in case there is something wrong with Duncan."

"Don't worry, that's fine. It doesn't matter who's looking after them, it doesn't stop us worrying does it? I'll nip to the loo," with that Francesca made her way to the ladies.'

She was walking on air. She couldn't believe what an amazing time she had had. Better than any of her dreams.

Murray glanced down at his phone. It wasn't from Graeme and he sighed a sigh of relief. But just as quickly as he had sighed, he went tense, noticing it was Rachel.

'Don't read it. Leave it till later. You're going to spoil this time with Francesca and you can't do anything and you certainly can't tell Francesca it's Rachel. She won't be happy. Just leave it and check it when you get home. It won't matter if you read it then, but it could matter if you read it now.'

He felt himself get really tense. 'Calm down man, think about Francesca.' He called the waitress and asked for the bill. He was paying it when Francesca bounced back. "Oh, are we going? Is something wrong?"

"No, yes, well, what I mean is yes. We need to get going. I promised my brother I would be no more than a couple of hours and I've just seen the time. So, if it's OK, I think we should go."

"Murray, what's happened? Is something wrong with Duncan, you seemed uptight suddenly?"

"No. I'm fine. Just need to get back." With that he helped Francesca on with her coat and led her out to the car.

Murray was quiet all the way home. Francesca tried to make small talk, but it didn't seem to help. So, in the end she sat and looked out of the window into the darkness, reliving the different conversations and whether she had said something that might have upset him. But she couldn't think of anything.

They drove up to Francesca's door.

"Thanks for a lovely afternoon, Murray. I've had a great time. I hope I didn't spoil it or do anything wrong. Oh, I nearly forgot. Here, I've a present for you."

Murray softened and turned and looked into her eyes.

"Francesca, I'm sorry. I've had a great time too. You were my saviour today. Your call and invite came just when I needed it most and it's been so much fun. Thanks, please forgive me. I just need to get back."

"That's OK. Here take your present and don't open it until the morning. Happy Christmas, Murray. Hope you have a great day. See you soon, and thanks again."

She gently kissed his cheek, quickly slipped out of the car and ran up to the door. He tooted his horn and was gone. She wasn't sure what had changed. For now she wasn't going to dwell on that, but rather muse over the last couple of hours of being in heaven.

Murray drove home, his mind totally scrambled. He felt bad he had left Graeme and Duncan all this time. He had loved being with Francesca. It had been such a relaxing and 'normal' afternoon and he'd been surprised at how little he had thought about Rachel during that time. There had been no heaviness or tension, no pressure to try and cheer Francesca up, or watch the conversation so not to cause any distress. There was a little bit of flirtation which came from both sides and was so nice. It made him feel human and desirable; but now he was on edge. Part of him wanted to read the message because he did have strong feelings for Rachel; he had longed to hold her and never let her go. But on the other hand he was tired, knew she couldn't give him what he wanted, and didn't think he had the strength to support both of them. So much of the support flowed from him towards her, until maybe one day she would be free to love him the way he wanted to love and be loved. Whereas with Francesca, they both had caring roles but during their rendezvous they had been able to relax, joke and converse on equal terms. It had been fun and oh how he missed having fun.

Chapter 17

"Hi there, I'm home. Sorry I took so long." Graeme and Duncan were sprawled out on the lounge carpet playing cars. Christmas music in the background, the tree lights ablaze in the window, and it appeared that there were now piles of presents under the tree.

"Hey, it looks like you've been busy."

"Yes, Dad. We had a good time. We playing cars." Duncan stated and Graeme laughed. "You OK, bro? Got everything done that you had to do?"

"Yeah, thanks, I'm fine. I'm just going to make a coffee, want one?"

"That would be great. In the meantime, I have some driving to do." And with that Graeme turned back and continued playing with Duncan.

Murray went into the kitchen and flicked on the kettle and as he did, he pulled his phone out of his pocket.

'Hi, Murray, I'm so sorry I was off with you. I'm in such a muddle with John not being well. I hope you have a lovely Christmas. I'll be thinking of you. Perhaps we can chat in the New Year when everything has settled down? Rachel.'

Murray found himself staring at his phone. The kettle had boiled and he hadn't even noticed. Poor Rachel. She's such a beautiful lady and yet so trapped. He felt guilty.

'I don't know. And then there's Francesca. What a great lass she is and such fun to be with. Laura, please tell me what to do. I'm so lonely without you. I feel abandoned, confused and worn out.'

"Murray, what's keeping you. Come-on, get yourself in here. Duncan and I are going to sit down and watch Cars DVD and we both think you should join us."

Murray dropped his phone on the worktop, made the coffee and wandered through to the lounge to sit and be with the two most important people in his life. The rest could wait but for now he felt Laura say to him, 'just enjoy what you have and let the rest take care of itself. Family always comes first.'

***

The afternoon had passed slowly for Rachel. The doctor had been in and checked on John. His breathing was more peaceful and it seemed that his temperature had come down. The doctor had instructed Rachel to keep him warm, supply him with plenty of drinks and encourage him to stay in bed. He wished her Happy Christmas and left, calling over his shoulder that he would look in after the Christmas break. And that was that.

John had slept most of the afternoon and Rachel had sat and cried for most of it. She didn't even have the energy to switch on the radio or television. She had never felt so alone. This was her punishment for what had happened all those years ago. The conversation with Father Ross the other day had helped console her. Indeed, the dream and realisation that her father should have taken responsibility, and by doing so, could have saved her brother's life. As well as the fact that she hadn't neglected him, but rather, had tried to help her mother had given her some absolution. However, the pain, tiredness, loneliness and the overwhelming feeling of having no worth or value was suffocating and squeezing any feeling of redemption from her.

She heard John call out and went to him. He smiled weakly and reached out and touched her hand. Then, with the smile still on his face, he closed his eyes again.

"John, would you like a cup of tea and a little piece of Christmas cake?"

"Yes please. That would be lovely." He whispered.

She slid her hand from his and went through to the kitchen. She saw her phone on the side.

Mmm, I wonder why Murray hasn't got back to me. He seemed really keen to talk to me before. I guess he's busy getting things ready and spending time with his brother and Duncan. Anyway, he probably doesn't need me now.

She made two cups of tea and sliced two small pieces of cake and walking back through to John, she decided she would sit by his bed and drink her tea with him.

***

Christmas Day came and went just like the day before. She had bought Christmas food and had planned to do a simple Christmas dinner for them both, but John wasn't up to it and she couldn't be bothered to cook for herself. In the end she made toast and banana for them both.

She had wanted to call Murray and just chat but knew that she couldn't. She sat with her phone in her hand mentally going through names in her head to see if there was anyone she could call and chat to. The only person she knew who would have time for her was Father Ross, so she dialled his number.

She sat nervously waiting, willing him to pick up the phone and yet at the same time she felt guilty that she was once again calling him and only because she was lonely and had no-one else to call.

"Hello there. Happy Christmas to you," came a cheery response. "Who's calling?"

"Happy Christmas, Father. It's Rachel Norris. I just, I mean I wanted to thank you for your help the other day and to wish you a very Happy Christmas. I'm so sorry to bother you."

"My dear Rachel, it is lovely to hear from you and you are never a bother. How's John?"

"He has been quite unwell. I had to get the doctor out on Christmas Eve but he seems a bit better today. He's just resting in bed and we're taking it easy."

The tears rolled silently down her face. Her heart melted as Father Ross chatted on. His voice was so warm and gentle washing over her making her feel snug and protected.

"I'm so glad you've been back in touch my dear. I know you're carrying a very heavy burden and since we spoke the other day I've remembered you in my prayers. You're never alone even if that's how it feels. God will give you the strength you need to cope. Just don't give up."

She smiled faintly. She felt so angry. Angry with God, herself, John, Father Ross and Murray. In fact with everyone. Life was so unfair. She started to sob, "Father, I'm so sorry to bother you today and to be so miserable. Please forgive me. I must go. I'm sorry I called."

"Rachel. Stop! Don't be sorry. I'm delighted to hear from you. I'm on my own today and needed someone to chat to and then you called so I am thankful. I sense you are angry about what's going on in your life at present. But my child, try and understand that it's OK to be angry. You're in a very difficult situation and it all seems unfair. Life is unfair. All of us in different ways come to realise this at some point, but it's what we do with that enlightenment that makes the difference. Don't dwell on what you've lost but think on all you have and had and be thankful. It won't change your circumstances but it will change the way you see things. Think about the true meaning of Christmas and how our blessed Mary the mother of Jesus must have felt in the end. I bet she felt life was unfair too." He chuckled.

"My dear, you and John are in my prayers and will continue to be. Feel free to call me anytime. Remember you've done nothing wrong. Be at peace and stop searching for absolution. Accept you're forgiven and draw on God's strength."

"Thank you, Father. Have a good day. Thanks for your advice. I'll give it a great deal of thought. Bye."

She finished the call, knew she should get up and wash her face, but she couldn't. All her energy had seeped away. She sat staring at the phone, pondering what Father Ross had said. Could she be forgiven? Was it possible to know and experience real forgiveness? She didn't even have the strength to pray, she just sat, tears poured down her cheeks just as if a dam had burst opened. Deep groans from way down inside erupted. It seemed to last forever. She couldn't stop it, in fact she didn't want to stop it. Rachel recognised this was all part of her healing and she knew she wanted to be restored and well.

She was suddenly aware that she was sitting in the dark. She'd no idea how long she'd been sitting there but felt calm and a little lighter in her spirit. "I must get up and wash my face and see to John." She said determinedly.

She strode into the bathroom, splashed her face in warm water and as she caught sight of herself in the mirror she thought she looked different. She turned and went back through and sat with John.

Chapter 18

Duncan had had the best day ever. Murray and Graeme made the day such good fun. They had opened all the presents, played games, eaten lots of lovely food, laughed and just enjoyed being together. Graeme and Murray had worked hard at making sure every moment was full so they wouldn't have time to pine for Laura. It didn't mean they didn't think about her or miss her, but they wanted it to be a day that she'd have wanted them to have, creating new, happy memories for the future.

Boxing Day arrived. Graeme had to leave and get back to work. Murray hated saying goodbye to his brother. They were so close, and the parting always tore at his heart. Today more than ever because they had had such a good time.

Duncan and Murray waved him off and wandered back into the house.

"Graeme gone, very sad. Please play cars, Dad."

"Yes of course, Duncan. It is sad, but we'll see him again soon. Come on, let's get that new remote-controlled car out and see what it can do."

They played for a while but Murray soon found he had had enough of whirling the car round and round the room.

"OK, Duncan, I'm going to go and make some lunch for us. You keep playing with your car and I'll give you a shout when it's ready. OK?"

Duncan was away in his little world, happily manoeuvring his shiny red car under the tree and past the sofa. Murray busied himself preparing lunch and an idea popped into his head.

I wonder what Francesca and Campbell are doing this afternoon?' Francesca has always been keen for the boys to play together; this might be a good opportunity.

He dismissed the idea and called Duncan through for lunch. As they sat in silence eating, he found the whole situation too quiet. *This is going to drive me mad,* he thought to himself.

"Duncan, how would you feel if I invited a couple of friends over this afternoon? You could show them your presents and play with them. Would you like that? We wouldn't miss Uncle Graeme so much then, would we?"

"Yes, I'd like that. Who's coming?"

"Let me see if they can come and then I'll tell you."

He texted Francesca. 'Hi, Happy Xmas. Hope you've had a good time. Wondering if you & Campbell are doing anything this afternoon? Appreciate you might be busy, but if not, Duncan & I wondered if you'd like to come over and help us eat the left-overs from Christmas Day!'

***

Francesca and Campbell had had a fun time with her parents. Her parents had made every effort to make it a day that revolved around Campbell and he'd coped with it amazingly well. On a couple of occasions when he got agitated, her dad had stepped in and taken Campbell out for a walk and when they returned all was well again. She was so grateful to her mum and dad. They'd been her rock since she found out she was pregnant, and ever since, walking with her through every heartbreak. Francesca and Campbell had stayed over Christmas night so she could have a drink and just be pampered by her mum for 24 hours — the best respite she could have.

She was packing all the presents into her car when her phone pinged. She couldn't think who would be messaging her today.

'I've spoken to all my mates and school won't be calling me to wish me a Happy Christmas and to ask after Campbell. I wonder who it is?'

She glanced down and her heart missed a beat. It was Murray. She scanned the message quickly and then had to re-read it because she was in shock.

"Did I read that right? He is inviting us round to his house for tea?" She muttered to herself.

'Wow, yes, he is.' She was all in a fluster.

"Mum, Dad, we've got to go. Thanks again for everything, talk to you later. Come on Campbell let's go."

"Everything all right dear? You suddenly seem in a bit of a hurry?"

"Everything is just great. I have had a wonderful time and I think it is just about to be complete. Love you both." And with that she drove off back to her house.

"Eh, Campbell, do you remember my friend Murray and his son Duncan? You've met them a couple of times and I've talked about them. Well they have asked us round for tea this afternoon. That'll be nice won't it?"

She crossed her fingers that were wrapped around the steering wheel. 'Please, please Campbell, don't throw a tantrum, please agree. I never thought this would happen. Please don't spoil this for me,' she prayed in her head.

Campbell sat looking out of the window processing what had just been said.

"You can take your new toys and show them to Duncan and you can see what he's got. It could be fun. And just think how much you would be helping him." Francesca waffled on, desperate for Campbell to agree.

They arrived at the house and emptied the car.

"Well, what do you think? I need to get back to Murray and tell him if we are coming. Please say yes, it will make today special, as well as yesterday."

"OK, but I want to take all my new toys with me or I'm not going."

Francesca couldn't believe it. On the one hand she was so excited, but the thought of carting all the presents back into the car and turning up with them all was so embarrassing. On the other hand, she knew if she didn't comply with Campbell's wish there would be no visit. So, she texted Murray. 'Hi there, how lovely to hear from you. We'd love to come. What time do you want us?'

Murray picked up the message as soon as it came through.

'Come as soon as you want. Duncan & I are just sitting about and would love to see you both. So whenever is good for you.'

Murray tidied up the kitchen and found the present Francesca had given him. He had forgotten all about it and must have put it down. He picked it up and tore open the paper. Inside was a bar of Lindt dark chocolate and a fridge magnet which said 'Friends are like chocolates, it's what's inside that makes them special.'

He stood looking at it. What a funny gift. I wonder how she knew this was my favourite chocolate. I'm sure that's never come up in our conversation before.

Chapter 19

"Let's go, Campbell, all the presents are in the back of the car. Can you grab that Yule log and a carton of juice from the fridge? It isn't nice to turn up to someone's house without something to give our hosts, is it?"

They drove to Murray's in silence; well, nearly silence. Francesca was humming Christmas carols and trying hard to keep to the speed limit. Not because she was worried about getting caught speeding, she just didn't want Murray to think she was that keen.

'I mustn't read too much into this and spoil things. He has invited us both round as a friendly gesture, I must relax and just have fun. Oh, but that's going to be so hard. I'm so very much in love,' she mused.

They arrived and parked. Campbell wasn't sure about all this, but he had noticed his mum was really happy and he didn't want to spoil things for her, so he decided to make an effort to be polite and friendly.

The bell rang and Murray dived straight for the door.

"Duncan, Campbell's here to play with you. We're going to have a good day, aren't we?"

Laughter filled the house. Francesca and Murray pottered around in the kitchen sorting out drinks and snacks while the boys played in the lounge. It all felt so easy.

"So how was Christmas?" Murray began.

"Great thanks. We went to my parents and they spoiled us. Campbell was on good form and I actually relaxed and had time chatting with my dad. He's always been someone I can talk to and just say how I feel and not worry that he will judge me. I think my mum and I are too alike and end up arguing. Well, probably I start arguing with her to tell the truth. Whereas my dad just listens and then when I've finished, he will say something funny and we laugh and everything feels better for a while. Campbell gets on well with both my parents, so it really does take pressure off me. How about you? Did you have a good time? When did your brother go?"

"Like you, we had a great time. Graeme is fantastic to have around. We always end up laughing about everything and he is so patient with Duncan. Graeme will play the same game over and over again and you believe he is enjoying himself. Whereas, manoeuvring an electric car round the lounge twice is enough for me. It drives me crazy. Then I end up feeling guilty and hating myself for not being more understanding of Duncan. So, having Graeme is great because he knows me, understands me and accepts me and does what he can to help."

Francesca was busy washing a few dishes that had been left in the sink.

"I know what you mean. The thing is, we live with our boys all the time and it can be hard and tiring. It's not that you've failed or that you're not a good dad. Murray, you are amazing, so kind and always cheery and you do your very best for Duncan. Don't put yourself down quite so much."

Murray turned and walked over to the sink. He took the tea-towel out of her hand, pulled her towards him and kissed her tenderly.

She thought she was going to faint. Not only had his actions surprised her, but the warmth of his body, the tenderness of the kiss and the strength in his arms that were wrapped around her, were totally overwhelming. She had dreamed of this moment for a lifetime and finally it had come true. Suddenly Struan's face flashed before her.

Where did that come from? She thought, and as quickly as the image came into her mind she pushed it away. Nothing was going to spoil this moment and she kissed him back with all the strength and passion she knew she had.

Murray was not as surprised about his actions as Francesca. He had dreamed of kissing Francesca since that afternoon they had spent together. The surprise was why he had chosen then, at the kitchen sink, with the boys in the next room?

But as he held her in his arms, feeling the softness of her skin and the warmth and excitement coming from her, he didn't care where they were or who was around. This was a moment he had been longing for and now he knew she was the girl he had been seeking.

"Mum, have you made us a drink?" Campbell called out from the other room.

Francesca moved away from Murray. "Yes, love. Just coming," and with that she picked up the two glasses of coke and took them through.

Murray stood, holding onto the sink as he gazed out into the back garden. A smile spread across his face. "This is a good day;" he muttered and busied himself making them both coffee. He wandered into the lounge where the boys and Francesca were sitting chatting about Duncan's new remote-controlled car. Murray watched as she chatted so easily with the boys, sensitive to how they responded. She was much younger than him and yet seemed so much more mature and so beautiful.

The afternoon went by in a flash. They all played games, watched a film, ate all the remains of the Christmas food and, for anyone looking in, they would have seemed like a happy, warm and connected family.

The house phone rang and Murray jumped up to answer it. It was Graeme just letting him know he had got home safely and all was well. While they were in conversation, Murray's mobile phone (which was sitting on the arm of the chair Francesca was occupying) rang. She picked it up and answered it without thinking.

"Hi, Happy Christmas," she said. "Hello, who is this? Do you want to speak to Murray? Sorry, he is on the other phone right now. Can I get him to call you back? Hello, who is this?"

There was silence. Nothing. It was obvious that, in spite of the silence someone was there, but not speaking. The phone clicked off and Francesca glanced down to see who it was. Murray walked in

"Sorry about that. It was Graeme just letting me know he got home OK," said Murray.

"You're popular. Here, your mobile just rang and I picked it up. Sorry I didn't think. It was an automatic response."

She handed him the phone

"No problem. Who was it?" He scanned the screen to see whose name flashed up.

"I don't know. They didn't say anything." She tried to sound nonchalant but in truth she was desperate to know, as her mind immediately went to Rachel.

Rachel knew that John had a chest infection and was poorly but she couldn't help wonder if she was at fault because of all the extra medication she had dished out to him over the past few weeks. Had that made him more susceptible to breathing problems? She also knew she could never tell anyone and that would just be another burden to bear.

As she pottered around in the house she prayed: "Please God, let John be OK. I promise never to leave his side again or dream of Murray or anyone. I will keep my vows and be the wife and carer he needs." But even as she said it, the overwhelming desire to speak to Murray rushed over her and she picked up her phone and dialled his number.

Oh no, I must have pressed the wrong number, she said to herself. That isn't Murray's voice. That sounds like Francesca from the Pop-In. But it can't be, I don't have her number in my phone. I mustn't say anything in case it is. But why would Murray be spending time with her on Boxing Day and why would she be answering his phone?

She dropped her phone and went to John to see if there was anything he needed. John started thrashing about in the bed and jabbering away making no sense. The phone slid onto the floor, but Rachel couldn't care about that — there were more pressing matters that required her attention. John needed her and she didn't know what to do.

"John, darling, what's the matter? Please lie still and let me get you some water." But John wasn't listening. Rachel reached for the house phone by the bed and called 111. She didn't know what was wrong, but she knew John was seriously unwell.

The ambulance arrived quickly and the medics took over. Rachel stood at the end of the bed looking on in silence as the events unfolded before her eyes. There was so much commotion, and before she knew it John was being moved onto a stretcher, wrapped in a blanket and being taken out into the ambulance.

"Mrs Norris, we need to get your husband to the hospital as quickly as possible. Would you like to get your coat and handbag and come with us? Don't forget your purse, keys and phone. Is there anyone you want to call to come and meet you at the hospital?"

"No," she whispered. "There's just me. I'll get my coat and bag. Now where's my phone. It was on the bed. Has it got caught up with John?"

"I don't think so."

Rachel rummaged over the bed and then looked down, scrambling around on the floor. "Not now, please give me a break. Where is it?" she cried out. She felt it under the edge of the bed, dragged it out, picked it up and rushed out of the door.

Everything was happening so fast. John had been sedated and wheeled into the ambulance. The blue lights had started flashing, one of the medics was talking into the radio giving details about John, and then they were gone. Rachel sat in the corner by the door, silent.

In what seemed like seconds, they were in the hospital grounds at the entrance of A&E. Rachel jumped out and followed on as the medics wheeled John through the doors and into a cubicle. A nurse appeared and said to Rachel, "Mrs Norris, would you take a seat in here for a few minutes until the doctor has seen your husband, then I'll come and get you and you can see him."

***

Rachel blindly followed the nurse into a small cosy room and just plonked herself into a nearby armchair.

Time seemed to pass too slowly. Every so often, Rachel could hear footsteps coming along the corridor and she would jump up and face the door expecting someone to walk in and tell her John was fine. However, more often than not, the steps would keep on going past the door. Eventually, a nurse entered the room.

"Mrs Norris, would you like to come with me and I will take you to see your husband? We've got him comfortable and I'm sure you would like to sit with him rather than be in this room on your own. The doctor will come in and speak to you both. Would you like a cup of tea?"

"Oh, thank you, that would be lovely." Everything seemed surreal.

Rachel followed the nurse through the swing doors passing some cubicles. Vaguely she heard people talking at the desk, but it was all a blur. The nurse jabbered on. Rachel merely smiled and kept walking. They reached the last cubicle on the right-hand side. As she walked in and saw John lying on the bed with eyes tightly shut and breathing steadily, she burst into tears.

The nurse took her arm, led her to the chair beside the bed and guided her into it.

"I'm so sorry. I don't mean to get upset," she reached into her pocket in search of a hanky. "I don't know what I'll do if something happens to John. It will be my fault all over again." She rambled on, not making a lot of sense.

"Mrs Norris, you've had a real shock. Now, you sit here with Mr Norris and I'll go and get you that cup of tea. The doctor will be here shortly."

The nurse returned with the tea, and was followed soon after by a tall dark young doctor.

"Hello, Mrs Norris, my name is Dr Mackenzie. As you know your husband was very agitated and unwell when the ambulance team arrived at the house. It would appear that he has had some sort of stroke. We are going to run tests and see how he goes. We will keep him in until we are clearer about what is going on. I appreciate this is a huge shock and a lot for you to take in. You must be exhausted, so I suggest you drink your tea? You're welcome to sit with Mr Norris for a while, but then it would do you more good to go home and get some rest. You're welcome to call the hospital in the morning and come in to see him any time. Obviously if there is any change this end, we will contact you."

Rachel couldn't take in what was being said. She just sat looking at this man standing in front of her and found herself thinking how white his coat was.

John. Stroke? How can that be? He had a chest infection. That was what the doctor had said the other day. They had had tea and Christmas cake earlier today.

She sat in silence for what seemed like an eternity.

"Mrs Norris, would you like us to contact anyone, or order you a taxi to take you home?" the nurse asked softly.

Turning to face the nurse, Rachel said faintly. "We don't have anyone to contact. It's always just been John and me. Is it my fault John is so ill? Did I do something wrong?" She stood up, the tea cup clattering against the saucer in her hand. She felt so fragile and vulnerable.

"Come on, let me help you. I'll take the cup and call the taxi. Once you've said goodbye to Mr Norris just come back through to the reception area and wait for the taxi. The driver will come in and call your name."

Dr Mackenzie jumped in, "Well, Mrs Norris, get some rest. Don't worry, we will do everything we can and see you tomorrow." And with that he left.

Sitting down without realising it she said robotically,

"Thank you, doctor," and with that Rachel reached for John's cold hand. She rubbed her thumb across his wedding ring and smiled weakly remembering the day they had bought the rings and had sat in a coffee shop trying them on just to see what they felt like. She pulled the blanket up under his chin and stroked his face.

"'Night, darling, sleep well. See you in the morning." And with that Rachel walked down the corridor and out into the waiting area. She had never felt so alone as she did in that moment.

The reception area was full of people, some with cuts and bruises, children crying and parents looking stressed and agitated trying to calm them down. There were even some sprawled across several chairs fast asleep. It was all so surreal.

"Norris, taxi for Norris." The piercing voice penetrated into Rachel's thoughts.

"Oh, that's me. Thank you," she stood up and walked over to the door. As she did, she was suddenly aware of a bell ringing in the distance. She walked through the door, into the night and followed the taxi man to the cab just outside the door.

Chapter 20

The rest of the evening had gone well, the boys had got along fine. Francesca and Murray had sat together on the sofa, a reasonable distance apart so not to give rise to questions, but close enough to sense their longing to be close, to touch and be touched by each other.

"Well, I think it's time we got going. It's been such a lovely day. Thank you, Murray, for having us and being a great host. Come on, Campbell. Gather up your stuff. Get your shoes and coat. We need to get home."

"Yeah I guess you're right. I need to get Duncan ready for bed and get things sorted for tomorrow. We're meeting up with a couple of Duncan's friends from the centre tomorrow. You're looking forward to seeing your friends again aren't you, lad?"

"Yes, me go to see my friends and take my new car to show everyone," stated Duncan.

"Don't know about that, let's see how things are in the morning shall we." And with that, Murray led the way to the front door and helped Francesca into her coat. He kept his hand on her shoulders. He could feel her tremble under his touch.

She could feel his hands squeeze her shoulders and desperately wanted to turn and wrap herself deep within his arms but knew she couldn't. Campbell was ready and waiting at the door looking at her intently. She knew the sign — it was time to get home. He had had enough.

"Thank you. That's us we're ready. Bye, Duncan, thanks for playing with Campbell and sharing your toys with us. It has been a lovely day, hasn't it, Campbell? Bye, Murray, thanks. Hopefully I'll see you soon."

She looked up into his eyes, leaned forward and kissed his cheek in a friendly fashion and headed straight out of the door.

"'Cheerio, Campbell, Cheerio, Francesca," shouted Duncan.

"'Bye," they called back in harmony.

"'Night, call you soon," Murray breathed into the night.

He closed the door. "Well, Duncan, that was fun, wasn't it? Have you enjoyed your day? Francesca and Campbell are very nice, aren't they? You wouldn't mind meeting up with them again, would you?"

"No, it was fun. I like Campbell."

"Great. We'll see them at the pantomime. Perhaps we can arrange to sit beside them, eh?"

With Duncan in bed, the kitchen tidied up and the house back to normal, Murray sat down and flicked through the TV channels. He picked up his phone and texted Francesca

"Hi, thanks so much for coming over today. It was so great. We both really enjoyed having you and Campbell. I just wish we had had more time on our own to talk. OK, I also wanted to hold you, kiss you and run my hands through your hair. Francesca, I know I am a lot older than you and neither of us have uncomplicated lives, but I think you feel about me the way I feel about you and if so I wondered if you'd be willing to come out with me again sometime soon so we can talk and be together? I appreciate you may decide 'no' and if that's the case, that's fine. Just let me know. Please don't mess me about. But on the other hand, if there's any chance you might be interested, I'd love to spend time with you. Take care, sleep tight and keep warm."

Suddenly he thought about Rachel. *I should call or text her and make sure she is OK. I always said I would be a friend to her and I can be that. I'll wait till everything is back into a routine, arrange to meet her and tell her about Francesca,* he thought to himself.

'Hi Rachel. Trust you had a good time over Christmas. I see from my phone I had a call from you. Sorry I didn't pick it up. We had a busy but surprisingly very happy time. Hope your husband is doing OK. Catch up soon. X'

Rachel sat in the back of the taxi, feeling totally numb. The taxi driver made pleasant conversation, but gave up.

The car pulled up outside her home, she paid the driver, got out, and let herself in. It all seemed so quiet and cold. She slipped off her coat and wandered into the kitchen to make some tea. Her mind was blank and she felt so cold. Just as the kettle was boiling, the phone rang.

"Who can this be?" She said aloud, as she picked up the receiver. "Hello, who's speaking?"

"Mrs Norris, this is Raigmore hospital. My name is Karen and I'm the staff nurse who has been looking after your husband. I really regret to tell you, but I have some very sad news. I'm afraid that just after you left, your husband took a turn for the worse, and I'm sorry, but he didn't pull through. He's passed away."

Rachel just froze. "What did you say? Is this some kind of joke? Who did you say you are?"

"Mrs Norris, it's Karen. We met earlier this evening when you brought your husband in."

"Oh, OK, thank you. Goodbye," she said robotically, and with that, Rachel put down the phone. She absentmindedly walked into John's bedroom, threw herself on the bed and sobbed.

Chapter 21

All the celebrations were over and the New Year started. The cold weather was still making its presence felt. All the Christmas lights in the streets hung there dull and unlit. In the main, the shops had removed all the decorations and sale signs were beginning to appear.

Louise was back at work and once again making her way down Chapel Gardens towards Chinwags for the Pop-In.

I wonder how many will turn up today? She filtered through her mind all the regulars and decided who would be able to get there. She knew that the chances were that the young mums wouldn't be able to come as the children would not be back at school yet. Then again, others might not make it because of the snow and ice. She would just have to wait and see.

The large wooden door was tightly shut. The bench outside all frosted over. Louise stood hunched up leaning against the door, hands tucked firmly in her pockets willing Margaret to open up.

She stood gazing at the patterns the frost had made on the bench.

So intricate. Each pattern totally unique. She lifted her eyes and looked up the street. So empty. So quiet. Funny to think a few days ago the place had been heaving with people.

How quickly things change and yet so much is familiar and shared by so many.

I wonder how many new carers I'll come into contact with this year. How many from last year will still be caring this year and happy to do so? How many will be exhausted and just want someone to listen to them? Louise mused. Another year has begun; there will be sadness and joy, laughter and tears and her job was to make sure that every unpaid carer she met was valued, loved, listened to, enabled and supported, in whichever way she could.

Mmm, what's my plan for this year? Do I still want to carry on in this job or should I look for a new challenge? She slouched by the door weighing it all up. Another organisation had offered her a job, but as Louise thought about those she was waiting to meet, she realised she was where she truly belonged. Louise wanted to help make a difference. After all, no-one knows when any one of us could find ourselves in that role.